Riptide

A SEAL COVE ROMANCE

ANNA BURKE

Bywater BOOKS

2026

Bywater Books

Copyright © 2026 Anna Burke
Library of Congress Control Number: 2025949344

Print ISBN: 978-1-61294-336-7

Bywater Books First Edition: March 2026

Printed in the United States of America on acid-free paper.

Cover designer: TreeHouse Studio

Bywater Books
PO Box 3671
Ann Arbor MI 48106-3671

www.bywaterbooks.com

*For anyone who's ever dared to ask,
'What if this time is different?'*

And, for Tiffany

Painter, printmaker, and theorist Albrecht Dürer (1525)
first described the logarithmic spiral—a shape often found in
nature, including the shape of some mollusk shells, such
as ammonites—and called it the "eternal line."

Chapter One

Dating and horses had more in common than Jen Alloway liked to think about. Both were romanticized, unpredictable, and liable to kick you in the chest. And the worst part? People kept going back for more, hoping the results would change despite the solid evidence—and bruising—to the contrary. Yet here she was, playing wingman to her friend Danny at a speed-dating event because that was what friends did. She'd even worn a nice shirt, not that she was expecting to meet anyone. It wasn't possible to form an accurate impression of someone in eight minutes or less, which was what this event promised. People could pretend to be anything for that amount of time.

"Are you sure I don't have something in my teeth?" Danny asked, tearing up a cardboard coaster as they sat at the bar of the brewery hosting the event. This was the third time Danny had asked the same question. Ollie, who owned the brewery and who'd been a friend of Jen's for years, snorted with laughter.

"You don't. You look gorgeous. Besides—you made me come to this." Jen chucked Danny under her chin. Jen wasn't worried about Danny. Everyone loved Danny. It was impossible not to. She was cute, funny, smart, and had a real gift for bringing people out of their shells. Playing wingman was the least Jen could do after

Danny's messy breakup.

"Anyway, I'm glad you're here, Jen," Ollie said.

"What? Why?"

Ollie grinned into their beer, which wasn't at all suspicious. "No reason."

"You have to tell at least me," said Danny.

"Nope. I think I'm gonna see how it plays out."

"Dick," said Danny, pouting.

Jen's shirt felt suddenly tight across the chest. "You didn't set me up, did you?"

"Me? No." Ollie, whose concession to fashion was wearing a *Storm's-a-Brewin'* brewery T-shirt without holes, wiped down an already clean tap and gave her a sly smile that failed to reassure. "Just relax. Try to have fun. Have another beer."

"Ollie." This wouldn't be the first time a friend had tried to play matchmaker. She didn't mind exactly, as it meant they cared enough about her to worry about her happiness, but she didn't need the help. When she found the right woman, she'd know. It had always been that way for her. If for the past few years the right woman had failed to materialize, well, that was just the way of it.

"A small one. I'm driving this one home."

"Because you are an angel." Danny patted Jen's cheek. "And I am a lightweight."

"I've got a batch I'm testing with a lower alcohol content that you—" Ollie glanced up mid-sentence, distracted. Jen turned to follow their gaze and nearly spilled her beer. She'd thought everyone had already arrived, but no.

A willowy brunette paused in the doorway of the old barn before crossing the concrete floor to join the assembly. Her business casual outfit fit her just right—navy blue pants subtly flattering her curves without giving everything away, though there was a sheerness to her white blouse that tightened Jen's throat.

"Damn," said Ollie. "Respectfully."

"I'm fucked. I can't talk to women who look like *that*," said Danny.

Blood rushed in Jen's ears as the woman hugged the brewery's co-owner, Stormy, without looking around. Something had gone horribly wrong with her voice box.

"You're just as hot, cupcake," said Ollie. "Relax."

Jen didn't say anything. She studied the woman's walk: confident, but with an edge that suggested the confidence was practiced, and a sway to her hips that wasn't. Jen tried not to stare too closely at the woman's ass. The dark blue slacks ended above her ankles, showing off low black pumps and an expanse of fair skin that explained why women's fashion had hidden that bit of anatomy for years. Jen wanted to hold that ankle in her hand and gently pull off the shoe, brushing her thumb over the delicate arch, which was an entirely inappropriate thought.

Ollie poured Jen another beer with an impish grin and slid it next to her. "You look thirsty."

"Don't even."

Ollie's grin intensified. "You both should probably go over there now. Thanks again for coming."

Danny grabbed Jen's hand and tugged her off her stool to join the crowd of attendees. Jen followed, attention still glued to the brunette, currently chatting with Stormy. Jen had hung out with Stormy a few times. She was good people. If this woman was a friend of Stormy's, that spoke volumes—and it suddenly mattered to Jen very much that this stranger was good people. Which was silly. Still, the air in the brewery felt heavy in her lungs, like she'd been sucked deep underwater. She focused on her breathing.

"Ahhhh, why did I do this?" Danny asked in a whisper.

"Because you deserve to have fun and meet people," Jen told her, steadying her voice. "Everyone is going to love you."

"Oh my god, what if my first date is with *her*?" Danny's whisper veered into a squeak.

"She's lucky then," said Jen, because that was what good wingmen said. They certainly didn't suggest that Danny swap places with Jen just because Jen's eyes were stuck to the woman like a burdock. Maybe she and Danny would hit it off. That would be good for Danny. She rolled her shoulders and tried to ignore the way the overhead lights brought out the chestnut hues of the woman's hair.

"I believe this is everyone who registered," said Stormy, patting the object of Jen's interest affectionately on the shoulder, which elicited a light ripple of laughter. "Thank you so much for coming to what I hope will be a regular series of events. My brewing partner, Ollie, and I are delighted to have you all, and we are going to have a fabulous time tonight.

"As you can see, there are two seats at every table. Those of you looking for multiple partners will have to sort that out later." She winked. "The rules for tonight's first activity are simple. Each table has an exhaustive list of speed-dating 'get to know you' questions and a set of dice. Roll the dice, answer the questions, and get to know the gorgeous folks who turned out tonight!"

At least the questions would be provided. That was something. Jen could carry a conversation, but without a horse to focus on, she was never quite sure what to say.

"Oh fuck," said Danny when Stormy counted them off. "It is with her."

Jealousy jolted through Jen. "You've got this," she said, hoping none of it leaked into her voice. "Just be yourself. She'll love you."

But hopefully not too much. Jen slipped her hand in her pocket and rubbed her good-luck fossil, which had been a gift from her father on her sixteenth birthday, and which she'd carried in her pocket ever since. The fact that she hadn't lost it was proof enough to her that it worked.

She watched Danny cross the floor to where her first date waited and then forced her eyes to her own table where hers sat. The other woman looked Jen up and down, grinned, and said, "I'm not into mascs, but I like your vibe. I'm Ash."

They ended up talking about motorcycles for their eight minutes, which was a pleasant warm-up. All the while, Jen was aware of the brunette at her table talking to Danny. Danny's worries, as usual, were baseless. She spoke animatedly, and her date seemed amenable enough. Jen couldn't quite smother the persistent pang of friendly jealousy. *She* wanted to be in Danny's seat right now. She continued to study the woman as surreptitiously as she could in between conversations. During each date, Jen tried to give her partner her full attention because nothing was as disheartening as thinking the person you were speaking to was waiting to talk to someone else, someone more exciting, someone with legs that went on for days beneath the table—

Focus. She rolled the dice and played the game.

Finally, the object of her distraction was next. The woman looked up at her with the loveliest pair of brown eyes Jen had ever seen—a light, almost amber color flecked with green, but not quite hazel. Eyes like blown glass.

"I'm Jen," said Jen, holding out her hand.

The other woman didn't take it right away. Those incredible eyes took Jen in, and then she blushed and hurriedly shook Jen's hand. Jen's confidence soared. She'd been checked out. Thoroughly. Her whole body revved with an interest it hadn't shown in months, and she couldn't bring herself to let go of her date's hand once she'd clasped it. The other woman's palms were soft and warm. Hands like that deserved worship.

Jen was not, however, a creep, and so she kept her cool—to an extent. The sheer blouse was low enough that each breath revealed the swell of breasts beneath. Jen determinedly did not so much as glance at that extremely tantalizing expanse of skin.

"Kate," Kate said, and nodded at their clasped hands. Jen's scarred and battered ones looked particularly rough next to Kate's, which were clean and smooth. "You obviously work with your hands."

"Is that a bad thing?" Jen asked. And, more importantly, was that a come-on?

"No." Kate's blush deepened. Christ, but she was attractive. The glow of the industrial-chic lighting above the seating area cast her in rose gold.

Jen gave her hand a gentle squeeze and looked at her unblemished knuckles, ghosting her thumb over the backs. She didn't miss Kate's quiet inhale, and couldn't help an equally quiet chuckle in response. It felt good to know she flustered Kate as much as Kate flustered her. Maybe tonight wasn't such a terrible idea after all.

"I work with horses, and occasionally—worse—goats."

Kate laughed, but something in her face shifted, putting out the sparks of interest growing between them.

"Which aren't you a fan of?" asked Jen.

"Oh, I love horses. Goats, too. What kind of work?" Kate's voice bore the slightest hint of strain. Interesting.

"Farrier," said Jen, hoping it wasn't the wrong answer.

Kate smiled widely with obvious relief, which was even more interesting. Jen made a note to ask her about that later if she could find a way to bring it up.

"That certainly explains it." Kate turned their hands so that Jen's was on top. "Do you normally let your clients chew on your fingers?"

Jen eyed her bruised pinky. "I actually gave that to myself off the clock with a hammer."

Kate brushed the damaged digit, no doubt noting the mottled blue and green blooming beneath the nail. "Were you building something?"

Jen dropped her eyes. "I do a little blacksmithing for fun, and I'm building a cabin. Between those two I don't remember which did it, but it was definitely a hammer."

"Did you say you're building a cabin?"

"I did." Jen's gaze flickered up and then stayed, a smile joining it as she searched Kate's face in turn. "I'm done with the exterior at this point. It's the interior that's giving me trouble."

Kate leaned forward, those luminous eyes bright. "How big

is the cabin?"

"Fifteen hundred square feet."

"You can do a lot with that size. What are you thinking? Open concept? You could do two bedrooms easily, or a loft. Sorry, I'm rambling." She gave a self-deprecating laugh, but Jen shook her head.

"Please continue. I've got plans, but I've been having a hard time visualizing what it's going to look like on the inside if I'm being honest. My brain doesn't work that way."

"I'm in real estate," Kate explained, "but I also do a little design. Small spaces are my niche."

"Come solve my problems?" Jen didn't want to release Kate's hand, but felt she had to, soon, in case Kate felt trapped. "What do you charge for your services?"

"Nothing yet. I'm ... I dabble, but ..."

"I make weird-ass sculptures out of old horseshoes. Your passion is at least practical."

"Practical. Hmm." Kate chewed on the word for a moment, and Jen regretted her choices. *Practical* could be misconstrued as boring, which was not her intent at all. "Tell me about your sculptures."

"Mostly it's tool repair or knives and bottle openers for friends, but sometimes—" She reached into her pocket and withdrew her keys. Dangling from one end was a small metal harbor seal. Kate picked it up.

"This is—well, stunning, actually." She turned it over to see the round belly and gently curving flippers, then sat it in her palm. Jen found the weight solid and comforting, and hoped Kate did, too.

"My friend Danny named him Bo. I've no idea why."

"Bo." Kate returned the keys with apparent reluctance, tapping the seal on the head once before relinquishing her grip. "He's remarkable."

Now it was Jen's turn to flush.

"Are you from here originally?" Kate asked.

"Rockport, but I had a cousin who lived in Seal Cove, and I

liked the area. Met Ollie through him actually. Brewery folks all know each other."

"I didn't realize there was another brewery here."

"There's a craft brewery every five yards these days. Not that I'm complaining. What about you?" asked Jen.

"Freeport, originally. My sibling and I moved to Portland after college, but I didn't like the city."

"Just the one sibling?"

"Cam's plenty," said Kate. Jen filed away Cam's name. "What about you?"

With a rueful grimace, Jen said, "I'm the middle of five."

"No wonder you seem so chill. My parents had twins their first time and decided that was enough."

"I bet. Were you trouble?"

"No," she admitted. "Cam was. I was the good twin. Boring."

"You're the least boring person I've talked to tonight," said Jen.

"That can't be true. Isn't someone here a rescue diver?"

"Aside from boring, which is obviously not true, how would you describe yourself?" Jen withdrew her hand from Kate's reluctantly and linked her fingers together on the table to prevent them from reaching out again.

"Practical."

Jen winced. She'd been right—that *had* been a poor word choice on her part. "You forgot funny, kind, smart, and talented."

"You don't know me well enough to know those things about me."

"Call it an educated guess."

Kate's eyes flashed in amusement. "Shall we play?" she asked, rolling the dice and finding the corresponding question. "Would you want to be famous and, if so, in what way?"

"Being famous sounds like a lot of work."

"Not even a little famous?"

"Well, if it's a little famous . . ." Jen indulged her. "Something crazy, like chaining myself to a bulldozer in protest."

"Seriously?"

"Yeah, why not?" Jen asked.

"You'd martyr yourself for a cause then?"

"The right cause, maybe, sure. Would you?"

Kate shrugged. "I think my talents lie in organization. A lot less glamorous."

"You haven't seen me try to do my taxes," said Jen. "But really, what would you want to be known for?"

It was strange how easy it was to forget she was in a room full of people as she waited for Kate's reply. The renovated barn with its stainless-steel brewing tanks faded into the background.

"Architecture."

"The next Frank Lloyd Wright." He was the only architect Jen could name, so she hoped that was a compliment.

"Only if we're dreaming. Your turn."

Jen turned the dice over in her hand, then rolled. "What are you most grateful for in your life?"

Kate answered swiftly. "My twin, Cameron."

"Are you close?"

"Probably too close," Kate said ruefully. "They're way too comfortable telling me things."

"Family." Jen raised her glass.

"You?"

"My friends. You've met one of them actually. Danny. She's the little blond. Ollie, too."

"Were you dragged to this as well, then? Not that Stormy dragged me. I was happy to come out and support—"

"Switch," called Stormy before Kate could finish. Jen could have tipped one of the giant brewing vats on her friend. She wanted to continue this conversation. Movement appeared at the periphery of her vision.

"Excuse me, sorry to interrupt," said the next date, standing awkwardly to one side.

Jen ignored them in favor of giving Kate her best smile. "Nice to meet you, Kate."

Most of the people Jen talked to after Kate were lovely. She hit it off with a few, but her awareness of Kate never faded. Sometimes she thought she felt Kate's eyes on her, but when she glanced over—whenever polite—Kate was paying attention to her current date. Jen uncharitably wished each of Kate's dates an urgent bathroom visit.

"The second and final activity," Stormy announced upon the last round's completion, "is a short game of queer culture trivia."

Jen tuned out the rules. Her last date—a high femme with sharp interest in her gray eyes who had made it very obvious she was down for whatever Jen wanted—had rested her foot against Jen's beneath the table, and Jen wasn't sure how to extricate herself. If she left her foot there, it would give the woman the wrong impression. If she pulled away, the woman would feel rejected, and Jen didn't want to be the cause. Thankfully, Stormy counted them off by six and ordered them to push their tables together, necessitating they move before Jen had to make a decision. Her body buzzed with the beer and the memory of Kate's hands in hers.

She gave Danny a one-armed hug when she popped up beside her. "You got group three, too?"

"No, but I switched. Having fun?"

"Surprisingly, yes," said Jen. Her eyes slid to Kate, who had joined their cluster. Seeing her, she started to say, "There's a seat next to—" but the butch from Jen's first date took it before she could finish.

"Hey bud," said Ash. "Any luck out there?"

Kate took a seat opposite. A smile, small and self-contained, curved her delicately made-up lips. Jen glanced up from Kate's mouth, realizing her gaze had lingered for longer than was polite. Was Kate's smile deeper now?

"Maybe," Jen answered Ash. "You?"

"I'm shit at this stuff." Ash rolled their neck. "Your friend seems cool."

Kate? No—Ash meant Danny, sitting at Jen's other side.

"She's the best," Jen said. "I'm here as her wingman."

"You're not looking for anything?" Ash gestured at the room. "There's gonna be some disappointment out there about that."

Jen laughed. Ash wasn't wrong. Quite a few of Jen's partners had seemed reluctant to end their conversations, and she'd caught a few lingering looks her way.

"I'm open to whatever."

"You're so chill, dude. I'm jealous."

"Hazard of the job." She didn't explain to Ash how working with horses meant she needed to exude calmness and confidence at all times for her safety. Horses fed off emotion worse than dogs—or maybe the results were usually more dramatic than what happened with dogs. Dogs couldn't kick you into next Tuesday.

Stormy passed out a piece of paper and pencils to each table. Jen caught Ash staring at Kate and felt her sense of camaraderie die a short and fiery death.

"Ready?" Stormy asked the group.

"Yes," they chorused back.

"Question one. Is Taylor Swift bise—just kidding." Laughter came from the tables. "Tragically not the bisexual queen we need, but what rising bisexual pop star wishes you all *good luck, babe*?"

"Duh," said Danny, jotting down the singer's name and holding it up for the group.

"Love her," said Everest, a woman with gorgeous curls and an equally curvy figure. Jen might have been interested in her had she not seen Kate first. Everest was one of the pairs of eyes that had lingered on Jen tonight, though their conversation had been stilted.

"I have no idea who that is," said Ash.

"You haven't heard of her?" Danny leaned around Jen to ask Ash. "You'd know it if you heard the song."

"Maybe." Ash's vibe suggested they didn't listen to much pop music, but they were clearly eager to impress Danny—and Kate.

"I wish she'd come to Portland," said Everest. "Though I'd drive to Boston or New York if I could get tickets."

Jen let the conversation unfold around her and glanced back at Kate. Kate must have felt her gaze because her eyes flicked up from the pencil she twirled between her fingers. Jen smiled. It was easy to smile at Kate, especially when that flush returned to her cheeks the longer they held eye contact.

"... don't you, Jen?" Danny asked.

"What?" Jen jerked her eyes away from Kate's and scrambled to remember anything she'd overheard. Something about the pop star, or maybe they'd moved on to beaches that allowed dogs. She wasn't sure. She hazarded a guess and said, "Yes."

"See?" Danny said to Ash. Jen hoped whatever point she'd backed Danny up on wasn't going to bite her in the butt later. An acceptable risk. She was generally chill—*guilty as charged, Ash*—but even for her it would be mortifying to be caught out so blatantly. Maybe she could have played it off, tried to act as if she were confident enough to be perfectly content showing her hand, but then Kate might have thought Jen was cocky and lost interest. And there *was* interest. She wasn't just imagining it. Unless she actually was cocky, in which case ...

She forced her attention back to the moment, trying to stop spiraling. She wasn't normally this distractable, even when she liked someone. Or maybe it had just been a long time since she'd had a strong reaction to anyone and she'd forgotten.

Stormy was speaking again. Jen needed to get her head out of her ass and pay attention, or she was going to look like an ass in a second.

The trivia questions were largely pop culture-related, though a few delved into queer history. Jen guessed wrongly on most of them, earning friendly teasing from the table.

"Someone needs to drag you out from beneath your rock," said Everest, her tone implying she was willing to do it herself.

"But I like my rock."

"You're *my* rock," said Danny, a giggle in her saccharine tone. She hadn't been kidding when she'd announced she was a lightweight.

"You two obviously know each other," said Kate.

"Jen was my neighbor growing up," Danny said. "Mutilated my Barbies. Cut off all their hair."

"You still made them make out with each other," said Jen.

"Well, duh. I was a baby gay."

"Do you live near each other now?" Kate asked.

"No," Danny bemoaned. "She wouldn't buy a duplex with me, so she lives thirty whole minutes away. Can you believe that?"

None of their compatriots could believe it and told Jen so. Laughing under the barrage of well-intentioned scolding, Jen stretched, her back sore from a day of work. Kate's eyes trailed over her body, and Jen's grin deepened—as did Kate's blush.

Yes, she was very glad she'd come tonight after all.

Kate traced the spiraling ammonite tattooed over the pulse point in her wrist and felt her heart fluttering with something like panic. When was the last time she'd cared this much about the outcome of a date? Her ex-fiance? Surely there had been at least one date in the eight months between then and now that had made her feel something. There had been that woman several months ago with the Rottweiler who'd been funny and sweet, though that hadn't ended up going anywhere, and then there had been . . . She searched her memory and came up blank. A nervous laugh slid past her lips and she clamped them shut before anyone else heard.

Too late she'd remembered the risk of attachment. To want someone was to make oneself vulnerable to loss. Adrenaline twisted her organs in its grip, sending a shockwave from sternum to gut. She'd forgotten what this felt like. How could she have forgotten? How could this twisting, knifing awareness have ever left her memory? Unless it was like childbirth, a pain the mind quietly tucked out of sight so that you dared to let your guard down again. Her heart, which had functioned just fine until this evening, pounded erratically. She didn't want this. She didn't want this at all.

Jen stood at the bar, talking to the brewer and a woman with phenomenal hair, the latter of whom irrationally annoyed Kate with her proximity to Jen. Talk about unsubtle. Kate couldn't tell if Jen was interested in the other woman or just being polite. The woman obviously thought the former.

Kate wasn't so sure. Jen had treated all her dates with the same respect and laid-back kindness she'd shown Kate. True, she hadn't held onto any other hands—that Kate had seen—but in retrospect maybe Jen hadn't known how to extricate herself from Kate's grip without hurting her feelings. Awkwardness was far more likely than interest.

Their eye contact, though; that had to be real, right? She wasn't imagining the chemistry? She wished Cam had come. She needed someone else's opinion and encouragement, and Stormy was busy. The paper she was supposed to use to indicate which dates she'd want to hear from grew damp beneath her sweating hand.

She gave herself a vigorous mental shake. She normally wasn't this insecure, but then again she hadn't actually wanted anyone in quite some time. Stakes had been low.

All she had to do was circle Jen's name.

But Jen might not put *her* down.

The thought of that rejection stung her right below her breast-bone. She pressed a hand there, the pain physical. Jen laughed at something her companion said. Kate clutched her pencil, the charged excitement of the evening dissipating.

No. Kate liked Jen, and Cam would never let her hear the end of it if she didn't get her contact information. She was overreacting. She could handle small disappointments. If Jen didn't put her down, too, then that was that.

"Did you have fun?" Stormy asked her, materializing at her side with a hint of cinnamon wafting off her skin.

"You're incredible." Kate kissed Stormy's cheek, her heartbeat calming. "Thank you for putting this together."

"First I have to drag you here, and now you're thanking me? Meet anyone you liked tonight?" Stormy's eyebrows danced suggestively. "Any surprises?"

"I don't know," said Kate, her eyes sliding to Jen despite her best efforts.

Stormy caught the slip. "Yeah, I thought you'd like that one. Go you. She's a buddy of Ol's, and from what I could tell was way into you."

"You don't sound surprised."

"I plead the fifth." Stormy winked. "I had a feeling you'd hit it off."

"You're incorrigible." A smile twisted her lips despite the admonishment. Stormy was notoriously always trying to matchmake her patrons. Kate should have known she was at risk of the same treatment.

"Thank you. Did you put her down?" Stormy snatched the paper from Kate's hand and made quick work of reading the one-item list. "Thought so."

"You don't have to be so smug about it." Her smile broke free nonetheless.

"Oh, but I do. Come here. I want you to meet Ollie. Ols!"

Ollie slid out from behind the bar and walked toward them. Kate took in their short stature, tattoos, T-shirt, and dark curly hair and smiled.

"This is the friend I was telling you about," Stormy said by way of introduction. Ollie gave Kate a quick up-and-down and then rolled their eyes at Stormy.

"You nailed it."

"I know, right?"

Ollie turned their attention back to Kate. "Sorry for being rude. I'm Ollie, Stormy's brewer, and it looks like you met my buddy Jen."

Kate blushed for the hundredth time that night.

"I did. Nice to meet you. I'm Kate."

"Jen," Ollie called over their shoulder, interrupting Jen's conversation. Jen extricated herself with a polite smile and wove through the small crowd to stand with them. "Give me your paper."

Jen, like Kate, was forced to surrender her slip. Did Jen's cheeks redden, or was Kate looking too closely? Ollie glanced at it, raised a brow, then exchanged a wordless conversation entirely of eye contact and eyebrow quirks with Stormy.

"I love being right," Stormy said after another second of this. She took Jen's slip and flipped it over, then did the same with Kate's.

Each had only one name.

"You can go ahead and exchange numbers now," said Stormy. To Ollie she added, "You can say it."

"You're a genius," Ollie said begrudgingly.

Chapter Two

Danny bounced in Jen's truck the whole way to her apartment, buzzing about one of the women she'd met and the cats they'd end up adopting.

"Please stop," Jen said finally, laughing. "You're such a cliché."

"I can't help that I know what I want," said Danny with a coy smile that Jen knew had gotten her into trouble countless times before over their long friendship—usually the kind of trouble Jen had to dig her out of.

Jen cleared her throat, then said, "Ollie set me up."

"Wait, what?"

The clues, in retrospect, had been there all along. "I was wondering why Ol was being weird about me coming to this thing. They asked about five times even after I told them I promised you I was going. You remember the woman who came in late?"

"The super-hot one? Kate?"

The memory of looking up to see Kate walking through the door sent a jolt of adrenaline through her veins. "Yup."

"Wait, Ollie set you up with her?"

"They and Stormy thought we'd hit it off. I don't know the exact details." But she would find out. Jen had hung out with Stormy a few times at Ollie's place and liked her, and that brief exposure had been enough to convey a personality more than capable of getting her way.

"Why hadn't you told me this?"

"Because you were planning your U-Haul."

"Fair. Tell me everything now?" Danny widened her eyes and managed a puppy dog expression that would have softened Jen up if she'd needed convincing, but she'd always been going to tell Danny everything.

"I have her number. At the end, apparently we each only put the other down, so . . ."

"Rude. I put her down, too." Danny's pout was nearly as adorable as her pleading face. Jen appreciated Danny's ability to bend the world to her will with the sheer power of her eyes and lips. It was useful, and often resulted in free drinks for them both. Danny had once confessed to practicing in front of a mirror, which Jen respected. It was important to know one's strengths.

"I was thinking about texting her tomorrow."

"Isn't that a little soon? Though I hate that rule. It's so stupid to pretend you don't care."

"She's in real estate. I was going to ask for her help with the cabin." She pictured inviting Kate over to see the site, offering her coffee on the deck while they walked through, Kate with a notepad in hand, or maybe a tablet. She didn't know what architects used.

"Like, paying her?"

"Of course I'd pay her."

"But that's not a date," said Danny, brows nearly touching.

"It's an excuse for a date."

"You don't need an excuse. You can just ask her on a date."

"But I do need help on the cabin, and if there's chemistry—"

"I think as long as you're clear with her that it's a date and also a consult, that's fine."

Danny had a point. "How do I do that?"

"Say, 'Hey, I'd really like to see you again, and I'd also love your opinion on my rustic cabin where we could live happily ever after.'"

"I like the first part of that."

"Tell her you want to have her over and also ask her if she does consults? I dunno, man. Does she do it professionally? It's not like you're flush."

"She said architecture was a hobby."

"Then I think you can ask for her opinion and offer to pay. Tell her the deck has a nice sunset or something. Maybe you should do dinner first." Danny leaned back in her seat and closed her eyes, her hair bunching up at the back of her head where she slouched. Her eyes were drifting shut despite her excitement.

Meanwhile, anxiety rippled through Jen like folding steel, slow and hot. Should she ask Kate out for coffee first? Maybe. But she liked the structure of having something concrete to talk about in case things got awkward.

"What did you talk about?" Danny asked, covering a yawn.

"Eight minutes isn't much time. Mostly our hobbies."

"You told her you're a blacksmith, right?" Danny wrapped her hand around Jen's biceps and squeezed. "It's hot."

"I mentioned it."

"Good. Did you ask her what she's looking for in a relation-ship?"

"No. That would have been smart." What if Kate wanted something casual? Could Jen do that? Casual wasn't really her thing, but maybe she could make an exception.

The thought startled her. She hardly knew Kate and she was already considering exceptions to her rules? That was either a good sign or a really, really bad one. Laura, her ex, had liked to push Jen's boundaries, which was partly why Jen had ended it. She'd have to keep an eye on her willingness to bend.

"You should ask her that next time, make sure you're on the same page."

"I will, I promise."

≈ ≈ ≈

The young couple standing in the townhouse living room scanning the tasteful yet generic millennial gray décor turned to Kate expectantly, their eyes alight with hope.

"It's a great area for hiking, too," she assured them. Their car had several hiking-related bumper stickers on the back and a top rack fitted for kayaks. Starter homes were hard to come by in this economy, but the townhouses in this development were among the more affordable new construction on the market. If the couple were really interested, they'd need to put a bid in fast and high. This was the most excited she'd seen them yet.

"I love the high ceilings," said the woman. Her partner—Kate didn't see any rings—nodded in agreement.

"The floor, too. Duchess is going to slip, though." Duchess was their Aussie.

"I believe this neighborhood has access to several of the bigger trail networks. The school district is fairly good, too, if you do end up expanding your family."

A pang of bittersweet envy pierced her. That wouldn't do. She'd wanted a family with her ex, Morgan, but had known that raising kids with her would mean raising kids largely alone.

"What I love most about this space is its flexibility." Kate gestured at the open floor plan. "You can make the most of the light in here no matter how you set it up, but since you enjoy entertaining, I wanted to show you some layouts I mocked up." She opened her folder and laid several papers on the island counter. "Take a look."

This was the part of her job she loved: helping her clients imagine their futures, seeing themselves and their dreams in the walls of the houses she showed them. It was matchmaking in a way, and playing the housing market was like dating, with all its crushed hopes and highs.

Speaking of . . . Her phone went off along with her heart rate.

Was it Jen?

Cam: *Call me*

Disappointment needled her ribs. Normally she'd be happy to hear from her twin, and she was, but she wanted to hear from Jen more.

"Hey you," she said twenty minutes later when she was in her car and driving.

"You never told me about your dates," said Cam. "You were supposed to text."

"I was tired."

Cam huffed their disapproval. "So? How did it go?"

"Exhausting, honestly." She dropped the peppy real estate agent tone and groaned. "But . . ."

"But?"

"There was someone there I liked," Kate said, trying and failing to stifle her smile.

"Say more."

"Farrier, masc, sweet and funny . . . We didn't get to do too much talking because the time passed so fast, but you would have liked her."

"What's her name?"

"Jen Allo-something."

"Hang on." She heard the sounds of Cam typing in the background and knew her twin was internet stalking Jen. "You're fucking kidding. This is who you met?"

"I can't exactly see your screen."

"Dark hair, great smile, shaved sides, ripped to fuck? Works in Seal Cove?"

"That . . . would be her."

"She's fucking hot," said Cam. "Great reviews, too."

"Are you seriously reading her reviews right now?"

"If she's going to date you? Yeah, of course I am. 'Jen is so easy to work with, and my horses love her calm demeanor.' 'I won't ever use another farrier again—Jen is the best!' Sounds like she has a fan club. Lemme pull up her socials."

"Cam—"

"Let me work. This is what I do."

"And here I thought you moved numbers around for rich people," said Kate.

"I do that too, but first I stalk them so I know who I'm dealing with. Lots of pictures of her with her friends, she has a dog, nothing that says she's been in a relationship for at least a year. I'll check to see what she's tagged in."

"You're taking this way too far," Kate protested, but they both knew she appreciated Cam's sleuthing skills.

"I think she cooks. Extra bonus."

"Why do you say that?"

"There's a picture of her making pizza on a grill and another one of her in a kitchen making bread. Aww, she's good with kids, too. Is that . . . yeah, looks like she has a bunch of nieces and nephews. That's good. You want kids."

"Just because she's good with them doesn't—"

"She hasn't updated her LinkedIn in years, no surprise there, but she has a Facebook page for her business. Lots of likes, lots more positive reviews. I dunno, is she real?"

"She certainly felt real."

"Felt?"

"You know what I mean." The memory of Jen holding her hand made her press her palm to her chest, cradling it against her sternum. Cam didn't need every detail.

"I'll keep digging, but she gets my initial approval."

"You'll meet her if it goes anywhere."

"No shit." The protective curl of Cam's voice warmed her. Her sibling had always been protective of her, and had grown even more so since she'd broken up with Morgan. She would have resented the implication she couldn't take care of herself from anyone else, but from Cam it was okay. Cam knew what she needed, and knew she wasn't getting it. Cam also didn't want to see her heartbroken again any more than Kate wanted to see Cam hurt.

"Should I text her first? Or wait to hear from her?"

"What was the vibe? Do you want her to chase you?"

"I'm not sure." She turned the confession over the way she'd turned over Jen's metal seal, analyzing it from all angles. "I could chase if I wanted to."

"Yeah, but do you?"

"It might be nice to feel, I don't know …" She trailed off, unsure how to articulate the sensation building in her throat. She wanted to feel wanted. Everybody did, but if Jen was shy, Kate was more than willing to make the first move. If she had her preference, though, what would she rather have?

I want someone to want me with their whole self, nothing held back. I deserve that.

The thought was so clear it surprised her. Yes, she wanted Jen to chase her. She wanted to feel like the center of someone's world, like they couldn't breathe without her in it. She wanted her contact info to burn a hole in Jen's pocket until she couldn't help but text Kate.

"So let her chase you," said Cam, reading into her silence with unerring accuracy. "If she doesn't, she's a fucking idiot."

Chapter Three

Evening light filtered through the clearing, sliding along the trunks of the trees she'd felled and milled and stacked for construction. A stray beam lit up the glass in Annie's hand. Jen shielded her eyes against the glare. Ollie's wife sat in her usual chair on the half-finished deck with a cocktail and a puffy coat and vast sunglasses dwarfing her petite frame as she presided over the work. Danny, Ollie, and Annie occasionally joined her to help with the build. Ollie, Danny, and Jen worked; Annie reigned. The arrangement suited them all. Annie had tried to help several times in the beginning, but after Jen watched her struggle with a hammer, she pulled a chair over to the construction site and asked Annie to be the safety officer. Jen's dog, a brindled pit mix named Mabel, lounged at Annie's feet, assisting with the supervision.

"A little higher," Annie called out to Ollie and Danny as they wrestled with the top rail of the deck.

"Still?" Danny asked.

"Still."

"Use the level," said Jen, scooping up the tool on her way over. She'd taken off her sweater, and her shirt clung to her back with a light sweat. It was the perfect temperature for this kind of work, and the beers Ollie had brought from the brewery didn't hurt.

"This is easier than framing walls," Danny said as she adjusted the railing. "It's outside and it's sunny."

"Happy?" Jen asked her and ruffled her curls as she passed. She'd set her hammer down several minutes prior, which had been a mistake, seeing as now it was nowhere to be found. "Anyone seen a hammer?"

"On the railing farther down," said Annie. "Where you left it."

"Thanks, Annie." Jen crossed the deck again and snatched up her tool, returning to hammering in the flooring. She could have used a nail gun, but she liked the slow, steady pace of her hands. The solid thunk of metal on metal on wood filled the clearing like the woodpecker who liked to bang on the cabin stovepipe. She could hear it from her RV every morning, rat-tat-tatting through the canopy. Once she finished framing the inner walls, she'd hear it from inside, though there was also the plumbing to finish and the certificate of occupancy to acquire from the town, along with an extensive list of smaller to-do items.

As she hammered, her mind wandered. Her forge lay a safe distance away from the house. It wasn't much more than a large shed of rough-milled boards, but it was *her* large shed. Within, she'd been working on custom hinges and knobs all summer in preparation for the cabin's finishing touches. A large pile of split firewood nearby needed to be stacked, but that would have to wait until she'd finished the deck. So much to do, always.

And, as had happened more often over the past twenty-four hours than she'd like to admit to herself, once her mind finished scanning its to-do list, she thought of Kate. Kate, who she was going to text tonight. She'd wanted to do it in the morning, but that seemed overeager. She was glad her friends had offered a distraction.

"Hey, Danny," Jen said, pausing her hammering. "Come here for a second."

Danny dropped the board she was carrying and squinted up at Jen. Jen moved to block the sun from Danny's eyes, a courtesy she could provide her shorter friends, and hesitated.

"Yeah?" said Danny.

"I don't know what to say."

"You don't—oh. Wait, you still haven't texted her?"

"You told me to wait!" She shoved her hands in her pockets and balled her fists, fighting her rising anxiety.

"Oh right. Okay, well, what do you have so far?"

"What are you two whispering about?" Ollie asked.

"Jen's chickening out about texting Kate," Danny said.

"That's not—I was asking your advice, dickhead."

"Group huddle." Ollie beckoned them over, and Danny and Jen obediently clustered around Annie and Mabel, who took advantage of the situation to beg for a butt scratch. Jen should have just sent the text herself.

"Workshop time," said Annie, taking off her sunglasses to reveal her face. Her wide brown eyes, at odds with the prickly persona she projected to the world, looked Jen up and down and softened. "It's gonna be okay, baby."

"This is what I have so far." She pulled out her phone and showed them the draft text in her notes app.

Hey, it's Jen.

"This is all you have?" Danny raised her eyebrows, unimpressed.

"You know I'm bad at making the first move," Jen said.

"Yeah, and you normally don't have to." Danny pinched Jen's arm. "This is good for you. Say, 'Hey, it's Jen. I had a really nice time with you last night. Would you want to grab dinner sometime?' It's simple. And yes, I decided you should have dinner before you invite her over to the cabin, creep."

"Danny's right," said Annie. "Neutral territory first. You clean up all right. You do own clothes you haven't worn in the forge, right?"

Real suspicion laced Annie's voice, and Jen laughed. "I do."

"Then ask her out to dinner like a gentleman."

"Okay." Jen took back her phone and, in a real text message this time, with her friends peering over her screen, typed: *Hey, it's Jen. I had a really nice time talking with you last night. Do you want to grab dinner sometime?*

"Be specific," said Annie. "Say 'next week.'"

Jen didn't want to wait until next week, but that did sound more reasonable than, say, tonight. She made the change and hovered over the send button. "I sound like an idiot."

"You do not sound like an idiot," Annie assured her, before adding, "An idiot would invite her over to her unfinished cabin where the only bathroom is in her RV."

That was a valid point.

"Hit send," Ollie suggested.

Jen hit send and immediately thought of seven different ways she could have better worded the message. It was done, though, and now came the truly terrifying part: the wait.

Playing around with CAD software, her fat orange cat in her lap, was usually how Kate spent her evenings, and tonight was no exception. Her current project, not that she had funding, involved turning abandoned lots into green communities. She was intimately aware of the housing shortage, which, while not as intense in Maine as it was in other places, did affect the area around Portland and some of the hotter coastal towns. Driving from showing to showing gave her plenty of opportunities to study the decaying infrastructure littering the landscape. Some of the lots were owned by people who'd moved out of state and abandoned the property with no forwarding address, making it difficult for the city to repossess. Often, they had fines and liens and unpaid taxes, which, she maintained, could be overcome with the right funding. Cam was good at tracking people down, too. On a whim, she'd asked Cam to find the owner of an old garage on the outskirts of town, and Cam had located them within twenty-four hours, not that Kate was ready to make a purchase of that size quite yet. Her cat flexed his claws as he kneaded her legs through her sweats. She winced and scratched his neck beneath his collar, eliciting a deep purr.

Her phone chimed. She jumped, as she'd continued to do every time it had gone off today. Like most days, this happened frequently. Usually it was a client or another real estate agent. This time it was Cam. She checked her disappointment and opened the message, only for Cam to FaceTime her instead.

"Hey," she said.

"I didn't feel like texting," said Cam. They were walking through downtown Portland with headphones, buildings and pedestrians flashing by in the screen's periphery. Kate caught a glimpse of restaurant patrons sitting on red folding chairs outside a pizza shop.

"What's up?"

"I'm pissed."

"I can see that." Cam's normally smooth features were scrunched with anger. Kate's heart clenched with sympathetic pain. "What happened?"

"My fucking landlord."

"Fist-bump Sam?" Sam, Cam's older landlord, seemed to think fist bumps made him more relatable. Predictably, it had the opposite effect.

"He sold the house."

Cam lived on the second floor of an old Victorian. They'd been renting the place for five years now and loved it. Kate loved it, too, with its gorgeous hardwood floors, tall windows, and ornate trim. It suited Cam.

"I'm so sorry. You can afford to rent someplace else at least. When does he want you out?"

"Two months. December 31st."

"Happy New Year," said Kate. "I'll check MLS for you and see what's out there. Why's Sam selling?"

"Some developer made him a cash offer."

"People usually fall for those," said Kate, mentally scanning the listings she knew of off the top of her head. None were good enough for her sibling, but they were a start. "Let me send you some possibilities. Do you want anything different?"

"Yeah, a landlord who isn't a dick."

"What if you bought a place?"

"Buy?"

"Yeah. You can afford a decent neighborhood. I'll send you some options."

"Sure. I just can't believe he wants me out in the middle of winter. I hate moving in winter."

Everyone hated moving in winter, but Kate didn't think that would be a helpful comment and so kept it to herself. A notification popped up on her screen before she could offer further consolation. An unknown number had sent her a text, but in the preview, she saw the first line: *Hey, it's Jen. I had—*

"Oh," she exhaled, unable to keep the surprise from her voice.

"What?"

"Sorry, I—Oh my god. She texted me."

"The woman from last night?"

"Yes. She wants to take me to dinner next week." Her cheeks heated as she stared at the message, Cam's face a small icon in the corner of her screen. Their expression brightened with her news.

"What are you going to say back?" asked Cam. "Besides yes."

"I don't know. I only just got the text."

"Do you need restaurant recs?"

"I'm not going to Portland so you can stalk my date, Cam."

"Be nice to me. I'm homeless."

"You are not homeless. I will find you someplace to live, and I will tell you how the date goes."

"Fine, love you."

"Love you too. I'm so sorry about your apartment."

"Thanks."

They hung up, leaving Kate to cradle her phone in her hands, Jen's words staring up at her, full of promise.

Chapter Four

Jen's RV closet was approximately the size of a school locker. She stared at her options, phone held in one hand.

"I'm taking her to The Grove," she said to Danny, who was on speakerphone.

"That fancy Italian place on the water?"

"Yeah."

"No offense, dude, but can you afford that?"

"It's not a problem." She had some spare cash from her latest job, and this was the best use she could imagine for her extra funds.

"I wish you'd let me dress you," Danny whined.

"I'm wearing the green button-up you like."

"With jeans?"

"With jeans."

"That's fine I guess."

"You guess?"

"What about a jacket?"

"Who cares about the jacket?"

"You should for starters. Do the leather or that canvas one."

"Do you have my wardrobe memorized?" Jen asked her, grinning as she laid out her clothes.

"Someone has to be the femme in your life."

"You know that being butch or whatever doesn't mean I have no fashion sense, right?"

"In general? Yeah. For you? No."

"Ouch."

"You burn everything! Why don't you have forge clothes like a normal person? Coveralls, an apron!"

"I have an apron."

"Well maybe you need one with sleeves!"

"Then it wouldn't be an apron. Listen, I gotta run, but I'll text you after."

"Take her home with you."

"You know I don't do that on the first date," Jen said, though the idea was certainly appealing.

"Prude."

"Hardly." Jen examined her reflection in the mirror and smoothed her ponytail. She'd been to the barber recently, at least, and the sides of her head were neatly shaved, the edges crisp.

"Well, go have fun then. Don't do anything I wouldn't do."

Jen snorted. "Yeah, okay." There wasn't much Danny wouldn't do when in the right mood, something that occasionally worried her.

Forty minutes later she was at the restaurant, early, and sitting at a table by the window facing the door. When Kate arrived, she'd know. She'd turned down the waiter's offer of a drink, opting to wait until Kate arrived, something she regretted as the minutes passed, ticking closer to seven, and her nerves grew. She hadn't had a reaction as strong as the one she'd had to Kate in a long time. Years, possibly, and maybe not since her ex. The soft glow of the overhead lights and the flickering candles weren't enough to soften her worries. She sensed Kate was someone she might be willing to put herself out there for—hell, she was here, wasn't she?—but that carried the risk of rejection. She could handle rejection, but that didn't mean she wanted to.

Six fifty.

The door to the restaurant swung open for what felt like the twentieth time, admitting a nicely dressed older couple. They were seated nearby and ordered a glass of red wine each.

Six fifty-five. Sweat pricked her armpits.

Her phone rang.

"Hi, Jen, it's Kate." Kate's voice was harried, and there was the sound of traffic behind her. Jen swallowed a premonition of disappointment.

"Hey, are you okay?"

"My tire blew out on 27."

Jen stood, flagging down the waiter and mouthing "emergency" as she sidled out of her seat. "Do you need help?"

"I can change a tire, but I feel terrible. I'll be a little late—"

"At least tell me where you are so I can keep an eye on traffic."

"It's quiet—"

"But dark. Kate, I can be there in five minutes, but I'm not going to pressure you. Do you mind if I come keep you company?"

Silence hummed along the line, and then Kate consented with a sigh that sounded relieved. "I'm just past the nature preserve. You know that farmhouse along the curve?"

"Yeah, I know the one. See you in a few."

Jen drove only a little faster than the speed limit. It wouldn't do Kate any good if she got pulled over by one of the two cops in town, though she wanted to hit the gas.

She's a competent woman, she reminded herself. *She doesn't need you racing to her rescue.* Jen wouldn't mind racing to her rescue. The thought of Kate on the side of the road in the dark wrestling with a carjack and a spare tire filled her with an emotion she knew she hadn't earned. It was too soon to feel protective. On the other hand, a woman alone on the side of the road was a target, and Jen would be damned if she let anything happen to Kate after it had been Jen's idea to go out.

Her headlights streaked through the trees on either side of the road, stark blacks and the bright flash of reflectors marking her progress. She had tools in her truck if Kate needed them, and she could park behind, shielding Kate from harm.

She could imagine Danny teasing her about trying to white knight Kate. It wouldn't be far off. Jen could change a tire in five minutes flat. If Kate needed her services, she'd be more than willing to oblige, but she didn't know Kate well enough to know if she'd welcome rescue or reject it. Some people were prickly about that sort of thing.

A car appeared on the opposite side of the road precisely where Kate had indicated, a shape crouched on the asphalt beside it. Jen turned around in the nearby farmhouse's drive and pulled in behind Kate, rolling down her window to the chill October air to call out, lest she startle her. Her headlights bathed the scene in white light, and Kate stood to shield her eyes.

"Fuck me," Jen muttered as she froze halfway out of her truck. Kate held a wrench in the hand not shielding her eyes, a thin silver bracelet falling in a brilliant arc. She had to be freezing in that sleeveless dress. Jen made herself move and shut the truck door, leaving the lights on for illumination, and already shucking off her jacket.

"Thank you," Kate said, a self-deprecating smile on her face. "I had it under control, but the light is helpful. I was using my phone flashlight and it wasn't going well."

Jen draped the jacket around Kate's bared shoulders without asking. Up close, she could see the gooseflesh running over Kate's pale skin, made paler by the contrast with her dark dress. Jen couldn't tell the color in the monochrome lighting. What she could tell was that it fit Kate perfectly, and her elegantly coiffed hair had to have taken considerable time and effort to arrange. Wind gusted around them, loosening several strands.

"Do you, um, want me to . . ." Jen gestured at the tire.

"Are you implying I can't change a tire?" Kate said, pulling the jacket on fully. The dress bared her calves, and the low heels on her feet couldn't be coping well with the gravel on the side of the road.

"Never. But you're dressed up, and I'm happy to do it." Jen put out her hand for the wrench. Kate held it out of her reach.

"Could you watch for traffic for me?"

Jen hesitated. It didn't seem right somehow to let Kate bend down in the dirt. On the other hand, the image of Kate holding a wrench in heels was doing something dangerous to her nervous system. "Of course."

Which meant Jen had to watch as Kate crouched down again, head bent as she loosened the lug nuts on the tire. One gave her more trouble than the others, and Jen twitched, longing to take over and spare Kate the hard ground on her knees. That fair skin had to be pebbled with rocks and red from the abuse. Jen could imagine far too perfectly how Kate's knees would feel beneath her hands.

"Motherfucker," Kate swore under her breath as she loosened the nut with a final wrench. Jen laughed. The curve of Kate's back straightened, and she stood, nuts arranged carefully on the ground.

"Do you have a jack?" Jen asked.

"Right here." Kate pulled the metal contraption out from the shadow of the car and placed it beneath, inserting a screwdriver into the handle for more leverage. Jen was impressed; then scolded herself. Of course Kate was competent. She was more than competent. Jen watched as Kate wound the jack, face tight with concentration, Jen's leather jacket reflecting light from the headlights. The dress hugged her hips. One foot was silhouetted by the glare, the Achilles tendon limned with white fire and the shoe slipping ever so slightly off her foot. Jen swallowed.

"Can I at least help you with the tire?" Jen asked when the car was lifted sufficiently and Kate stood panting. A strand of hair lay against her neck, and the thin chain of a necklace glinted against the collar of the borrowed jacket.

"Fine," Kate said, her smile half in shadow. "If you insist."

Jen had rarely felt so grateful to be useful. She muscled the flat tire off the axle and rested it against the back of the car, which was open to reveal the spare tire in the bottom compartment. She lifted it out, aware that Kate was watching her and trying not to look like she was showing off.

Kate accepted the tire instead of letting Jen put it on. Was she making a point? Did she not want someone to take care of her?

Jen filed the information away for later.

Or perhaps, she amended as she watched Kate tighten the lug nuts, her jaw set firmly with effort, it was because Kate was almost as competent with a wrench as Jen. Another gust of cold wind blasted through Jen's thin shirt. She shivered and moved to block the wind from Kate's side. Up close, she could see Kate's hands as she gripped the wrench: the shine of nail polish; the angle of her wrist; the slow curve of her forearm with a splash of ink over her pulse point that Jen couldn't make out in the darkness. She'd touched that hand. Held it, even. Lit as it was now, the very idea seemed sacrilegious. Kate had worked hard to appear this elegant for Jen, and even in the gravel on the side of the road she was radiant.

"And done," Kate said, looking up at Jen with a satisfaction she didn't quite manage to hide.

So Kate *did* feel like she had something to prove. Interesting. Jen offered her forearm as Kate stood, and she did at least take that, letting Jen bear some of her weight as she righted herself. The jacket fit her well. Jen was broader, but it didn't hang off Kate's full frame. Jen wanted to smooth the leather over her arms and pull her into an embrace, which was entirely inappropriate given the setting and their level of familiarity.

"Do you still want to get dinner?" Jen asked, crossing her arms over her chest for warmth. Kate stepped closer and made to shrug off the jacket.

"Keep it for now."

"I have one in the car," Kate said, and slipped the garment off despite Jen's protests, draping it gently around Jen's shoulders. It smelled like Kate. Kate, who stood close enough to kiss now if Jen was feeling stupid. Jen relaxed her arms and let Kate settle the jacket to her liking, a slight frown wrinkling her brow as she adjusted it with more fuss than was merited. Heat filled Jen's cheeks. She was glad it was too dark outside for Kate to see how the care in the gesture affected her.

"I'm starving," Kate said. "I'd love to eat."

The restaurant was sympathetic to their cause, and the same waiter as before led Jen and Kate to a table lit by candlelight. Jen pulled the opposite chair out for Kate to sit. Kate's lips curved in an amused smile that stirred a flush in Jen's neck and brought a self-deprecating smile to her own lips as she imagined how flustered she must appear, which was only half as flustered as she felt.

"You—" she tried as she sat back down, knocking the table. "You're efficient."

She'd wanted to say gorgeous, but it didn't feel right. Not yet.

Kate's cheeks pinked as she tucked that stray strand of hair behind her ear. She'd pinned the rest up in a twist that surely had a name, but Jen wasn't well versed in feminine hairstyles and could only admire the way the smooth strands caught the warm light of the restaurant lamps like gold floss.

Then she saw the ammonite tattoo on Kate's wrist. The curving shell gleamed black and gray against her skin.

"Ammonite," Jen said, feeling like a bucket of slag. *Form a complete sentence, idiot*, she told herself.

Kate glanced at her. "I collect ammonites."

No fucking way. Jen didn't believe in signs or omens, but she couldn't deny this one. She pulled her good luck charm out of her pocket. The ammonite fossil her dad had given to her on her sixteenth birthday still fascinated her more than fifteen years later. "These little guys?"

"May I?" Kate held out her hand, and Jen set the fossil in her palm, her fingertips skimming Kate's skin for a brief, annihilating second. "Where did you get this?"

"My dad found it on a project site in England," said Jen. "He works construction and finds things at dig sites all the time. It's real."

"Look at this part here." Kate held the fossil up to Jen, leaning closer as she did so, with her fingertip touching the outer end of the spiral embedded into the rock. The fossilized ammonite stood out in relief. Jen had looked at it a thousand times, probably more, and the little head carved into the fossil to make it look like a coiled snake was an old friend.

Forget fossils. She could smell Kate's perfume this close: lilac and something darker.

"See the carved snake head?" Kate glanced up through her lashes as excitement laced her voice. Jen wasn't really supposed to be able to resist that, was she? "People used to think they were petrified snakes. They called them serpentstones."

Jen felt the strands of fate tighten around her as Kate spoke. This had to mean something—how could it not?

"My father always told me they symbolized the actions of saints." She remembered his gruff voice speaking gently as he pressed the stone into her hand. Jen hadn't followed her father's faith, but she'd felt the weight of his belief in that little fossil. It was a symbol of his protection, of his unshakable love. Nothing was holier than that.

"What made you choose an ammonite for a tattoo?" Jen asked. "Besides your collection."

The waiter arrived at that moment and they placed their drink orders, Kate opting for a cabernet sauvignon while Jen selected an IPA.

"The eternal line."

Jen blinked. That hadn't been what she'd expected to hear.

"It's a mathematical equation," Kate said, her cheeks pinking again. "It describes the spiral of a nautilus shell. Do you remember logarithms from math classes?"

"With horror," said Jen, who preferred the more applicable algebra.

"It's a logarithmic spiral. I always found it comforting, I guess. The way it curls ever inward. Maybe that doesn't make any sense. My grandmother used to take me beachcombing. It was one of the few things my twin wasn't into, so it became special."

"I remember—family is important to you." Jen's speech felt halted. Kate had her as stunned as a newborn foal. She couldn't take her eyes off the spiraling shell, imagining the needle inking that fair skin, solidifying Jen's fate long before Kate knew she existed.

"Do you want a family of your own eventually?" Kate toyed with the thin silver bracelet on her wrist, not meeting Jen's eyes. They were doing the hard questions then. Danny would be pleased.

"Yeah. I'd love that. Kids, too, if they're in the cards." Her nieces and nephews were the highlight of her life.

"Really?" Kate looked up and Jen was once again struck by the warmth of those eyes.

"Yeah. You?"

Did Kate want a family? That was a bit of a dealbreaker for Jen, and had, in fact, been what ultimately split up her and Laura. Laura didn't want kids or a domestic life, and Jen had tolerated that difference as long as she'd been able to.

"Yes." Kate sipped her wine and scrutinized Jen's expression as if she could read something more there. "I'm thirty-two. There isn't a whole lot of time left, you know?"

Jen knew plenty of couples who'd had kids later than thirty-five, but she didn't mention it, not wanting to invalidate Kate's fear. Besides, a vivid image of Kate holding a baby had leapt into her head, which was putting the cart way before the horse, but she didn't care. Kate would look good with a kid. She hoped she got her wish, regardless of who she was with.

"You said you were building a cabin?" Kate asked, changing the subject.

"I could use your advice actually. I'm framing the inner walls, but I'm rethinking my floorplan."

"I could come take a look. I mean—" Kate broke off, and now it was Kate's turn to look flustered. Jen's stomach relaxed. She wasn't the only one affected.

"I'd love that. I was going to ask you, but my friend—you met Danny—told me that was creepy."

Kate laughed. "I go to strangers' houses for a living."

Jen respected the hell out of that. It took guts to be a woman in most fields, but especially those where one was alone with a client and anything could happen.

"Still, I figured I should buy you dinner first."

"What makes you think I'll let you pay?" Kate tilted her head in a challenge.

"Please?"

Kate considered her. "I'll think about it."

"That's all I ask."

"I just feel like butch women—sorry if that isn't how you identify—always get stuck with the tab, which isn't fair. I can pay for myself."

"It's the least I can do when you look like that." Jen bit her lip. "Which came out wrong. I'm sorry, I—"

Kate laughed and reached across the table to take Jen's hand. "You're gorgeous, too."

Jen's entire body flamed. "I—" she stammered and stopped. Kate's hand was warm wrapped around hers. "Thank you."

"Have you been to this restaurant before?"

They discussed the menu for a few minutes, Kate's hand still on hers, and the waiter came by in due time for their order. Chatter from the other patrons rose and fell around them, and their own voices wove and mingled with the other tables, conversation flowing as easily as the wine.

"What's your least favorite date question?" Jen asked after a while.

"Oh, that's a hard one; I don't think it's the question so much as who's asking it, you know?"

"Fair. Do you date a lot?" It had to be asked, even though Jen didn't like putting anyone on the spot. Kate gave her that considering look again, a bit like she was a rusty lug nut.

"No, I don't date that much. I use the apps occasionally. You?"

"My friends usually drag me to a bar or something."

"I'll take an app over a bar," said Kate with a shudder.

"I bet." She knew what happened to women like Kate in bars, and other women could be every bit as predatory as men. "Why'd you go to the singles event? Stormy?"

"Yeah. She's a good friend, though I don't see her as much as I used to. My ex and I didn't stay friends exactly, and Stormy was her friend first."

"That sucks. I'm sorry."

"Thanks."

"How long ago did you break things off?"

"Eight months. It was my call." Kate paused with a frown. "No one ever tells you how hard it is to break things off with a good person."

"I hear you." Jen dared to stroke Kate's hand with her thumb. "I broke things off with my ex, too. We wanted different things."

"Yeah."

"Can I ask what happened with yours?" Jen probed, curious against her better judgment. "No pressure."

"She . . . Morgan is great, but her work hours were awful. I never saw her, and ultimately . . . I know it sounds petty, but I got tired of eating dinner alone, and I knew I couldn't ask her to change her job."

"What did she do?"

"She's a large animal veterinarian."

"No kidding." Jen didn't ask Morgan's last name. She was pretty sure she knew exactly who Kate was talking about. Morgan Donovan was the Seal Cove large animal vet, and a casual acquaintance. At this precise moment she was glad Morgan meant no more to her than that, or else she might have had ethical quandaries about dating a friend's ex. As it was, she had a surge of sympathy for Morgan, who had lost the woman now sitting across from her.

"What about you? Were you together a long time?"

"Six years," Jen answered. "We've been done now for three years, though."

"And you stayed single this whole time?" Kate's eyebrows were raised as she looked Jen up and down. "Really?"

"I had a few casual things that never went anywhere. I'm not the sort who'll jump into something just to have somebody."

Kate smiled at this, slow and surprised. "Me neither."

"To not jumping," Jen said, raising her glass in a toast.

"Or settling." Kate clinked her wineglass to Jen's glass of beer, that smile still on her lips.

"So what are you looking for?" Jen asked. "In a relationship, or whatever."

"Something real." The candle on the white tablecloth gleamed between them. "You?"

"Yeah. Something real."

Someone, she wanted to say, like you.

Jen looked devastating in forest green. Kate's fingers curled around the stem of her wineglass as she tried not to stare too obviously at the way the cloth stretched over Jen's torso, perfectly fitted to her shoulders, arms, and chest. It was too easy to imagine herself in those arms. By now, however, she knew that perfect chemistry didn't guarantee a perfect match. The person within that gorgeous body mattered more.

She liked what she'd seen so far. She wished, briefly, that Cam were there so that she could ask them what they thought of Jen, but the impulse faded as the night unfolded. Grease from the tire still stained her hands despite her attempts to clean it off in the restaurant bathroom. Jen had seemed impressed with her ability to change a tire, and she had to admit, that pleased her. She liked surprising people. She fixed things in her listings more than she'd thought she would as a real estate agent, and had acquired a small but useful skill set.

"What's something you've always wanted to do but haven't?"

Jen asked her.

"Is that one of Stormy's dating questions?"

There were so many things Kate had always wanted to do. She'd never gone skinny-dipping or ridden on a motorcycle. She'd never hiked anything more than a few miles at a time. She wished she read more.

"I want to get a degree in architectural design," she said after a moment. "I like real estate, but I want to do more."

"Like what?"

"Like design homes people can actually afford to live in that don't sacrifice quality or community. Most of what I do in real estate is matchmaking, but most people can't afford what they actually want or need, and there's so much real estate just sitting there going to waste. We can do better."

"What's stopping you from getting your degree?" Jen's open expression invited Kate to tell her everything.

"I might apply this year. I've had a lot going on the last few years and the timing hasn't worked out. Besides, I'm doing fine in real estate. I don't need to go back to school."

"Yeah, but if you want to, that's worth something."

"How did you become a farrier?"

"A program and then an apprenticeship, and I have an undergrad degree in animal science. I knew I wanted to work with horses but I didn't want to be a vet, no offense to your ex."

"None taken."

"I've always been better with my hands than my head."

I bet, Kate thought, glancing at Jen's hands. Their food had arrived while they talked, but she'd barely touched hers, so intent was she on Jen.

"There's a joke in there," Kate said softly, touching Jen's hand for the third time tonight. She couldn't seem to stop herself. The smoothness of the skin on top was a direct contrast to the tough skin of Jen's palms and finger pads, though scars marked that smooth surface in ridges. Jen's thumb skimmed over her hand

and Kate shivered, the touch almost more than she could bear. The delicacy of the gesture despite the obvious strength in Jen's body established a dichotomy Kate was suddenly quite desperate to explore. She wasn't used to desire striking like this—hot and sudden, the weight of it softening her eyelids and parting her lips.

"What was it like growing up with only one sibling?" Jen asked, and for a time they spoke of their families, exchanging anecdote after anecdote while Kate's body thrummed with a life she'd forgotten it capable of possessing. Jen's laugh thrilled her with its soft edges and rolling waves, and when her knee brushed Jen's beneath the table neither of them moved away. They ordered dessert and another drink, more, she thought, to stay at the table than out of any real desire for food, though the flourless chocolate cake was delicious. Jen spoke of her equine clients and their moods and whims; Kate told her about some of her wackier human clients with their unreasonable requests and expectations.

Then suddenly it was ten o'clock, and the waiter was bringing them their check with a subtle hint that the restaurant was closing.

"Do you want to take a short walk by the water?" Kate suggested, unwilling to relinquish the glow of the night just yet.

"Yeah," said Jen, her eyes brightening with the same eagerness Kate felt spilling out of her own gaze. "Will you let me pay? Please? I'd like to."

Kate didn't want to like that about Jen. She could pay for herself and wasn't one to expect anyone else to cover her tab. Usually she split the check. There was something so sincere about Jen's offer, however, that she relented. "Only if I can cover the tip."

"Deal."

They settled the bill and stepped out into the cool October night. The wind off the water was brisk—cold, even—and Kate wrapped her wool coat tightly around herself, wishing she were wearing more substantial clothing but determined to persevere.

"Are you cold?" Jen asked as they set off at an easy stroll along the town's edge.

"I'm fine," Kate lied.

"May I?" Jen put a tentative arm around Kate's waist, offering up her body heat. Her arm was firm and stable, and Kate was glad of the warmth as they approached the strip of rocky beach near the lobster dock. Moonlight sluiced over the water, obscured by the occasional shred of scudding cloud. They paused to listen to the breaking waves.

"I had a nice time with you tonight," Jen said after a moment of comfortable silence. "Tire change and everything."

Kate shifted to get a better view of Jen's profile, aware that she was now pressed more firmly against Jen than she'd been a moment ago and struck again by the swiftness of desire's descent. Jen's breathing quickened. Kate wouldn't have been able to tell if she hadn't been standing so close, but as it was, she was sure Jen could feel the pounding of her own heart against her ribs.

"Me too," she opened her mouth to say, but instead of words, she reached for Jen's face, turning it toward her. Jen's cheek was warm despite the cold air. Jen's other arm wrapped around Kate's waist as Kate leaned forward, her heartbeat wild and her breathing erratic as she paused an inch away from Jen's lips. They stood frozen like that, breathing, until Jen's hand slid to the back of her neck and pulled her in.

God, if she'd thought her body alive before, it was nothing to this. Jen let her lead for a moment, her lips pliant and lush beneath Kate's, but when Kate parted her lips for more Jen squeezed her waist and pulled Kate flush against her body, deepening the kiss with a certainty that fell as a blow to Kate's knees. She leaned into Jen. Light blazed in her mind's eye. A quiet sound of longing slipped off her tongue and into Jen's mouth.

"Fuck," Jen said lowly, her hands sliding down Kate's hips and back to her waist. Kate felt the touch through the thick layer of her jacket as if it burned against her skin. She shivered. God, she'd forgotten what this was like, how entirely consuming you could find another person. Jen's teeth sank gently into Kate's lower lip and Kate whimpered again, pressing closer, tighter, eliminating the space between them. The kiss she returned was harder, more insistent. Jen's fingers laced through her hair and cradled her skull like it was precious to her. Kate, meanwhile, shoved her hands beneath Jen's leather jacket to cling to her back, the heat radiating from Jen's torso enough to ward off the chill. Her nails dug into the solid muscle along Jen's spine as she held on for support, and she felt Jen's whole body shudder in answer.

Jen pulled away first, panting. She leaned her forehead against Kate's. "Is this okay?"

Kate kissed Jen's neck, gently nipping the considerable bulk of her trapezius and daring to taste her. Jen's gasp was her reward. She pulled back to say, "Yes," not that she felt the word particularly necessary when her body so clearly wanted everything Jen had to offer. Then, with a monumental effort, she forced herself to slow down. This was a second date. More of a first date, really, since the speed dating had been so short. There were lines she didn't cross, not this soon, and she'd made a promise to herself she wouldn't rush into anything.

This was rushing, for all that she wanted it.

"It's okay," she amended, "I started it. I should have asked you."

"I think it's pretty clear it's okay by me," said Jen.

Kate kissed her slowly, but only for a moment. Jen let her pull back with obvious reluctance. "Kissing is as far as I'll go, though, for a while, so if that's a problem—"

"Definitely not a problem," said Jen.

"No?"

"No." Jen's eyes strayed back to Kate's mouth. "You've clearly never kissed yourself."

Kate's laugh was blown away by a vicious gust of wind. They both pressed instinctively closer together.

"Do you want to head back to the cars?" Jen asked.

"No, but we should." Kate leaned into Jen, resting her cheek against Jen's jaw for a few heartbeats while she gathered up the remnants of her willpower. Jen's arms wrapped around her. No one had held her like this in a long time. It unlocked an almost desperate grief as her heart demanded *more.*

"You've got to be freezing," Jen said into her hair. "Come on."

"Mm," was all Kate managed. Jen smelled like clean laundry and a subtle cologne, but she could imagine all too well how she'd smell coming home after a day of working with horses and iron. Her pulse hummed at the thought. She did, however, allow Jen to lead her back to their cars, where they kissed again before parting ways for the night. Jen had an early morning, and Kate didn't think getting into Jen's truck was a good idea. It would be all too easy to not get back out.

"I like you," Jen said bluntly as she held open Kate's car door. "Can I see you again?"

Kate touched Jen's face. She couldn't seem to help herself, nor could she help her smile. "Only if it's soon."

Chapter Five

Kate pulled into the long dirt drive and checked her GPS. This was the address Jen had given her, and the site matched her speculations. The road had been put in recently, judging by the raw stumps lining the path and the signs of disturbed earth, and the new-growth forest loomed on either side in the October evening. Night fell so quickly now. It surprised her every year.

She wore jeans and a blue knit sweater against the chill, a far cry from the dress she'd worn the other night, but significantly more practical. She'd also brought her tablet and a growler of Storm's-a-Brewin' beer. There was no reason for her palms to be sweating aside from the agony of wanting. One real date wasn't enough to get to know a person. So much could still go wrong, strangling the hope brewing in her chest.

She'd spoken to Cam about Jen, of course, which had only made things worse. She'd heard the excitement in her own voice as clearly as Cam had, and then Cam had the temerity to say "You haven't talked about someone like this since Morgan."

Surely at least one of the dates she'd gone on in the interval between her breakup and now had excited her. She couldn't pull up a single face, however, that thrilled her the way the memory of Jen's did. It was too soon to feel the way she was currently feeling, and while she'd thought she was ready for it, now that the emotions had her in their grip she was terrified. She'd forgotten how falling really was a plummet: one part elation, one part scream.

The road curved, and there at the end of the drive stood a log cabin Kate could sell for a significant sum. Jen had built that? Herself? Kate stared over the steering wheel at the deck with its rustic pillars and swooping descent, imagining Jen laying boards one by one. Kate spent a lot of time trying to make her listings feel like a home, and helping others see the potential for home even in the most dire circumstances. This, though—what would it be like to live in a house built with love and intention, home held in the mind's eye like a beacon?

Before she could spend too much more time in her own head, however, Jen emerged from the cabin and waved. Kate's heart leapt up her throat and she tasted metal as she tried to calm her reaction to Jen's simple gesture. The dog by Jen's side barked and wagged its tail but didn't bolt for Kate's car.

They'd kissed. Her lips tingled at the memory as she got out of her car, waving back. Growler in hand, she walked up the dirt drive to the front porch. Jen's smile washed away her nerves and replaced them with something almost worse in its intensity: anticipation.

"Hi," said Jen, hands now in the pockets of her jeans and an old blue flannel shirt snug across her shoulders. Casual suited Jen. Kate felt better about her choice of clothing. "This is Mabel."

Mabel wagged her tail and approached at a half-crouch, ears flattened and face upturned.

"Hi. This place is gorgeous, Jen," Kate said as she bent to greet the brindle dog. Mabel sniffed her hands then rested her shoulder against Kate for scratches.

Jen spared a glance for the clearing, and by her rueful expression Kate guessed she was seeing the rough earth and stacks of timber, and not what Kate saw—potential.

"It's coming along."

"You built this yourself?" She touched the rail of the front porch, smooth where the bark had been peeled back from the pole, save for the dark knots.

"With help from my family. I think I told you my dad's in construction."

"How he found the ammonite."

"Exactly. Come on in. I have a fire going. It's brisk out here." Jen held the door open for her and she stepped inside.

Jen hadn't been kidding about a blank slate. The outer walls had been framed, but there was nothing save support beams delineating the rest. The high ceiling emphasized the emptiness, but the last rays of the sunset streamed in through the large glass windows overlooking the slope of the hill down toward the road. A stone fireplace dominated one wall. Warmth radiated over the unfinished floors, and two camp chairs were pulled up beside the blaze, along with a folding table and a cardboard pizza box. Kate set the growler down beside it and turned to assess the space once more.

"Very open concept."

"That's what I was going for, definitely." Jen leaned against a support beam with a grin. "See why I need help?"

"I'm sure you could figure it out on your own, but since I'm here . . ." She stepped into the open, marking a line with one arm. "I would recommend the kitchen here and the living room here so that the eye flows from one to the other, and you could put a small guest room and bathroom in this space here. If you wanted to divide the living room from the kitchen you could put in a bar or an island." It was a simple layout, and one she was sure Jen could have come up with on her own, but Jen nodded as if this was all news to her.

"I wasn't sure how big to make them. I mean I have the original architectural plans, but . . ."

"Do you have the dimensions of the house?"

"Sure." Jen pulled a carpenter's pencil off a bit of framing and squatted on the subfloor to sketch. Kate knelt beside her.

"You have these memorized?"

"Looked at them often enough. Here."

They both stared at the numbers scrawled on the floor. Jen's handwriting slanted to the right, with an optimistic lift to the strokes.

"Typically, you'd consider a division here or here for the kitchen." She took the pencil from Jen, and with only a moment's hesitation sketched out several possible arrangements. "And the dimensions for a guest room really depend on how large you want the bathroom, but I recommend either this or this."

"I feel like I should be paying you for your expertise."

"Consider it a gift." Kate gave her a quick smile. "Will you show me your forge?"

Jen's forge was set back from the cabin in a building that could generously be called a large shed.

"Did you build this by hand, too?" Kate asked, taking in the rustic frame with its neat right angles.

"Built it before the house. It lulled me into a false sense of security."

"Building a house isn't like building a shed?" Kate teased.

"If it was, I probably wouldn't have built the house at all."

"It's lovely." And it was—simple yet sturdily built. It possessed a confidence in the way it overlooked the house, a sentinel of sorts, perhaps.

Jen flashed her a grin. "Here we are."

Kate stepped inside the door Jen held ajar and searched for a light switch. Her fingers found it quickly. The overhead shop lights cast their harsh fluorescent glow over the room, which was dominated by a vent hood and a setup that must have been the forge, judging by the soot marks on the steel drum and the remnants of hot coals. The rest of the room contained utilitarian shelves and workbenches. She wandered over to one and picked up a doorknob from a pile of knobs, admiring the curving shape and the solidity of the object.

"Is this for the cabin?" she asked.

"Yeah. Pretty much all the hardware over there is."

"I love the weight of it." She set it down and touched a handle, which still retained the nail holes of the shoe for character. "Are these all from your clients?"

"People know I collect them by now and they give them to me. Some are from my clients, yeah."

"Fond memories?"

"Hah. Well, some of them, yeah."

"Tell me about your worst client."

"Snowbell. That pony was maniacal. Size of a dog, but knew how to throw her weight around and had the fastest bite I've ever seen. There was no getting away from it."

"Size is deceptive. Will you show me how it works?" She gestured at the forge, still turning the handle over in her hands.

"It's a wood burner, so it will take a minute."

"A fire sounds nice." Perhaps she shouldn't press Jen to perform. For all Kate knew, Jen had anxiety, though it didn't seem like it with the easy way she stood by the forge. "You don't have to if it makes you uncomfortable."

"Uncomfortable?" Jen's brow furrowed, the very concept apparently foreign. "I don't want to bore you."

"Do I seem bored?" She stroked a finger down a hinge before raising her eyes to Jen's.

"I—" Jen stammered. Her eyes dropped to Kate's lips. Kate smiled but didn't go to Jen—not yet. The memory of their first kiss still seared along her nerves. She wanted to savor it, and to savor the tension thickening between them.

"Please?"

"Okay," said Jen, her eyes still soldered to Kate's mouth. The glare of the shop lights softened on Jen's cheekbones, forgetting its fluorescence. Kate was about to take a step toward Jen, resolve be damned, when Jen turned to busy herself at her forge. She gathered wood from the stack by the wall and lit a fire, working quickly and efficiently. Kate pictured her holding a horse's hoof with the same care and felt a swelling tenderness between her ribs. Mabel, who had followed them into the shed, leaned against her leg.

When the fire was underway, Jen slipped an old horseshoe into the coals. They chatted idly while the shoe heated from black to, at last, a bright cherry red Kate wanted to pop into her mouth. The color was juicy and enticing, despite the air around it shimmering with heat. Jen rolled up her sleeves. Kate tried not to stare at the blue-green veins beneath Jen's skin or the rippling of her tendons.

"How do you know when it's ready?" Kate asked.

"It's about there now. See this color? This is what I'm looking for." Jen reached for the shoe with her tongs and placed the hot metal on the anvil. "Shoes start out a bar, like those on that shelf over there. Sometimes I'll bend them back to a bar when I'm reusing them. I like the curve of this, though, so I'm going to keep pushing it."

She picked up a hammer and tapped one end of the shoe. The metal sagged and shifted, bending beneath the blow. "This is a cross-peen hammer. It's what I use for most of my hobby work. My rounding hammer, which I use for shoes, is in my truck with my portable forge."

"A portable forge is kinda sexy," Kate said, amused by Jen's immediate blushing response to her words.

"I'm having some people over this weekend," said Jen, changing the subject with a flash of a smile. "You should come."

Anxiety jolted through her body, followed by excitement. "Oh yeah?"

"Ollie will be there, and you've met Danny. I could invite Stormy, too. Just a small thing. We usually hang out on the deck, do a little work, have a few beers . . ." Jen smithed while she talked, striking the metal with smooth, sure strokes of her hammer. Kate watched Jen's shoulders, aware of the strength in Jen's body with each careful tap. God, but she was gorgeous. There was something elemental in her movements: the flex of muscle beneath her shirt, the hot burn of the coals, the metal shifting in her hands.

Half mesmerized, Kate said, "I'd love to meet your friends."

"You could bring your twin."

"Are you sure you're ready for that?" Kate stepped closer to the heat of the forge. Jen shoved the iron back in the fire and cupped Kate's jaw in a callused, gentle hand.

"I'd love to meet them."

Kate didn't intend to swoon. She was quite positive she'd never swooned in her life, but her knees softened and she wrapped an arm around Jen's waist to steady herself as Jen closed the distance between their lips with a burning kiss.

Her first client of the day was an old draft mare with a stiff hind end. Jen stroked the mare's broad haunches, speaking to her in soothing endearments as she eased the hoof onto the stand for the rasp. The mare kicked once, then allowed Jen to set her hoof down with a few clicks and pops in her joints.

"How are her feet looking?" asked the owner, a woman in her early forties who doted on the mare like a prize show jumper. Daisy the Percheron had the best home Jen could imagine for a retired workhorse—light hacks in the woods, the occasional drive harnessed to a light carriage, and plenty of horse cookies, massage treatments, and loving scratches to her hairy chin, which the horse adored.

Her feet, however, were not looking great. The mare was kept barefoot, but her hooves chipped and flaked, and they might have to try shoes on her if this continued, though Mary, the owner, was adamant about the benefits of barefoot trimming, which Jen found amusing. Barefoot trims worked great for some horses. Others needed a little more structure, especially in damp New England. Still, she appreciated the woman's dedication to her horse, even if she wished she'd listen to Jen's professional opinion.

"We may need to consider shoes," she said for the twentieth time as she worked the rasp over the toe in long, swift strokes.

Shavings of hoof drifted to the barn floor.

"Let's try a little bit longer," said Mary predictably.

"See here?" Jen pointed at the chipping wall of the hoof she held and launched into her explanation yet again. Her mind, however, was far away from the cool shade of the barn.

She hadn't asked Kate to stay the night before because she believed in taking things slowly, but she'd never hated her own principles more. That kiss—had she ever been kissed like that? The memory made concentrating on her current conversation exceedingly difficult. Kate kissed like a building storm, soft yet sure, the yielding warmth of her lips a soft roll of thunder through Jen's body. Kate had wrapped her hand around the back of Jen's neck with bold assurance, pulling her in and down. She felt the ghost of those fingers still. And Kate's hair, heavy in Jen's hands, running over her fingers in ripples and eddies—she cleared her throat and tried to focus her attention back on her job. Letting one's attention wander around horses was a surefire way to get hurt.

How could she focus, though, when the memory of the little sigh Kate had breathed into Jen's mouth rode roughshod over her consciousness? How could anything else matter when she knew the velvet softness of Kate's lips?

"...a trial period," she continued, "or you could try booties. I have clients who have had success with those on rougher terrain."

Kate liked when Jen's thumbs found the line between the smooth slope of hipbones and the plane between them. The rough, warm curve of horse hoof beneath her fingers wasn't enough to ground her in reality, now that she knew the way Kate felt pressed against her.

"Not now, Gaston."

Jen glanced up from her work to see a long-haired black tom sauntering down the barn aisle, tail held high as a flag as he fixed yellow eyes on Jen.

"Who is this?" Jen asked, continuing to rasp. All she had to do was even out the flare on the left and the horse was done. She finished in four more strokes and set the horse's hoof down off the stand, giving the mare a pat.

"Stray someone dumped. You know how people are."

Jen nodded. She did know how people were, unfortunately, and wasn't surprised. People saw a barn and assumed it would be a safe place for them to dump their unwanted animals, especially cats. Sometimes it was even true. Mary worked with a local shelter and often helped trap ferals. Gaston looked like he'd settled in just fine.

"He looks healthy." Scarred, with a nasty weal over one eye, but plump and sleek. "Is he intact?"

"Not anymore." Mary reached down to pet the cat. He rubbed his face vigorously against his leg. "But he's still terrorizing the other barn cats."

"He looks like a fighter." Jen stretched out her hand for the cat to sniff. Sad though Gaston's story might be, Jen's head was still too full of Kate to hold anything else. She scratched the cat beneath his regal chin, admiring his thick ruff of hair, and wondered if she could use him as an excuse to text Kate.

"Can I take a picture of him?" she asked.

"Sure."

Jen snapped several portraits of the cat. He blinked his eyes at her slowly. Friendly guy. Back in her truck, she pulled up one of the pictures and sent it to Kate, adding: *Someone dumped this handsome guy at a client's barn.*

Kate owned a cat. Therefore, she probably liked cats—Jen had been waiting for an excuse to text her all morning, not wanting to seem off-puttingly eager, but desperate to talk to her again. Her throat burned with suppressed words. She wanted to know everything about Kate: who she was, what she liked, and what she wanted from Jen. She was aware this could be nothing more than a passing obsession, a fling with perfect chemistry that would go nowhere, but it didn't feel like that.

"What if she's the one?" Danny asked her that night over a beer. "What if this is it for you?"

"Stop it," said Jen, waving away her friend's teasing. "I like her a lot, but we just met."

"When do we get to hang out with her?"

"This weekend actually. She's gonna come over Saturday with her sibling."

"You're meeting her family already?" Danny's blonde eyebrows knit together.

"They're her twin. I think they're best friends."

"They? Wait, what if we dated twins? You get Kate, I get her twin."

"You haven't even met them."

"It's the principle. Besides, Kate's hot. Therefore, so is her twin."

"Is that how that works?"

"Duh."

"Please don't hit on Kate's sibling," Jen begged.

"I won't. But I can't promise they won't hit on me," said Danny with wide-eyed innocence.

Danny finished her beer and set it down on the deck railing. Jen play-punched her friend in the shoulder and settled back to watch the sun set over the trees. Truthfully, she was more anxious about meeting Cam than she'd let on. Kate struck her as a woman who knew what she wanted, but she also clearly trusted her sibling's judgment. Kate might want her now, but that could change with a word from Cam. On the other hand, if Kate was willing to let Jen meet her sibling, surely that was a good sign?

Chapter Six

"Are you sure you want me to crash this party with you?" Cam lounged on Kate's couch while Kate got ready, looking long and lean in jeans and a dark blue button-down. How Cam managed to find clothing that minimized their mutually curvy hips was a mystery to Kate, but Cam had found a way to fit to their identity the body the two of them shared. Kate shimmied into her jeans with a little hop to pull them up over her hips.

"I'm sure."

"It's gonna freak your girl out, you know that, right?"

"Not after she meets you."

"You don't think I'm intimidating?" Cam raised an eyebrow, not a hair out of place. "Ouch."

"You don't have to come if you don't want to."

"Shut up."

The invitation had slipped so naturally from Jen's lips—surely there wasn't too much anxiety underlying that confidence?

"She won't think you're a test, will she?" Kate asked Cam.

"I mean, I am." Cam, upon seeing the look on Kate's face, amended her words. "Look at it this way: you'll get this over with. It's not like she's meeting our parents. I'm a softball. Unless you want me to play hardball . . .?"

"Absolutely not."

"Then choose a shirt so we can go."

Kate's nerves grew the closer they got to Jen's place. She'd made a mistake in bringing Cam. Making Jen nervous had not been her intent, but what if that was what she'd done?

"Stop chewing on your lip; you've ruined your makeup," Cam chided her.

"I can't wait until you start seeing someone," Kate muttered darkly.

Cam laughed. "Not likely. I'm homeless, remember?"

"You do know there is a real housing crisis, right?"

"Sorry, sorry, poor taste. I'm still pissed about my apartment."

"You could always move in with me."

"Not with that commute."

"You like driving. Exhibit A: this is my car and you're behind the wheel."

They continued their gentle bickering until Jen's driveway, at which point Kate's tongue became intrinsically attached to the roof of her mouth. Should she apologize to Jen? Or would that draw attention to an issue that maybe wasn't even there?

Stop it, she ordered herself. She was a grown woman. She knew what she wanted. Cam was easy company. Everything would be fine.

Jen stepped off the deck at their arrival and greeted Cam with an outstretched hand and Mabel's enthusiastic full-body wiggle.

"You must be Cam," Jen said, smiling at Kate. "I can see the resemblance."

"And I've heard a lot about you," said Cam, intentionally making it awkward before pivoting. "Your place is gorgeous. I love living in Portland, but I could go for something like this. Is that cedar decking?"

"Good eye," said Jen. When Jen dropped Cam's hand, she turned toward Kate, clearly unsure how to greet her in front of her sibling. The brief flash of uncertainty in Jen's eyes loosened the knot of Kate's own anxiety. She reached out and squeezed Jen's hand, stroking her thumb over the scarred skin, then entwined their fingers together. Jen's smile widened, and the nerves Kate had briefly glimpsed seemed to vanish. "Everyone's on the deck."

"Everyone" consisted of Stormy, Jen's friend Danny, and Ollie and their wife Annie. Stormy enveloped Kate and Cam in a hug, pinching Cam's cheek in the process with the admonition to "Stop being so handsome." Kate also didn't miss the way Cam's eyes lingered on Danny, who looked adorable in jeans and a flannel shirt with her curly blond hair framing her round face. Perhaps Kate should have seen that coming.

"We're the work crew," said Danny. "I've personally nailed in at least four of these boards."

"More than that," said Jen, still holding Kate's hand. Kate decided she wouldn't mind holding onto Jen's hand all night, counting the burn scars across the backs, the warmth between their fingers chasing away the October chill. "At least seven."

"I'm actually quite devastating with a hammer," Danny continued.

"I don't think we've met before," Ollie said, introducing themself to Cam with a grin of queer recognition. "This is my wife, Annie."

The introductions continued around them. Jen's hand stayed firmly entwined with hers. When she caught Jen's eye, the smile she received was shy and sweet, and something terminal happened in Kate's chest, a sort of wrenching stab that journeyed from the lips Jen had kissed to the soles of Kate's feet.

"Hi," she said for Jen's ears alone.

"Hi."

"Thanks for having us."

"It's a real hardship," Jen said with an arched brow. Kate had never quite figured out how to raise her own eyebrows and mildly envied Jen the motion even as she laughed at the depth of her sarcasm.

"Still."

"Can I get you something to drink?"

"In a minute," said Kate, aware that Jen getting her a beverage would mean Jen leaving her side, and feeling deeply reluctant to part with her yet. The warmth of her presence drove away the loneliness hiding around the edges of her usual contentment, and she wanted to bask in the glow a little longer. Jen pressed their fingers closer together. Did she, too, feel that longing for proximity? Kate glanced at Jen again and found her doing the same. They shared another smile, which was ruined only slightly by the snort of laughter Danny covered with a cough as she turned to address them.

Eventually, however, Kate did let go of Jen long enough for Jen to seat her and Cam in two of several freshly constructed Adirondack chairs, which Danny was quick to point out she had *not* helped build, and therefore would probably hold their weight, though Kate was beginning to suspect Danny was more than capable of light construction. Jen brought them cold bottles of beer. A metal firepit cast warmth across the deck.

"Kate tells me you're in finance," said Jen, looking at Cam. Danny perked up on the other side of the circle of chairs.

"Yeah, but I'm not a finance bro. I won't bore you talking about the market."

"You can be *such* a finance bro," Kate teased them.

"You *do* ask about market forecasts."

"It's relevant to my work," Kate said with a toss of her head. "I have to."

"What do you do?" Cam asked Danny.

"I'm an ER nurse."

"Badass."

"She is," said Stormy, patting Danny's knee with pride. "Nothing, and I mean nothing, freaks this girl out."

Danny's cheeks pinked under the praise, and Kate tried not to roll her eyes at Cam's obvious interest. Her sibling was too predictable sometimes.

The talk turned to building the cabin, with each member of the "work crew" chiming in to tell stories about all the mishaps, most of which featured Jen in various embarrassing—and endearing—straits.

"And that is why they decided they needed a safety officer," Annie said primly. "Someone needs to have their hands free to call 911."

"Yes, that's totally why you became the safety officer," said Danny with an eye roll. "Certainly not because you nearly brained me with a hammer."

"It's not my fault you were standing behind me."

"Wouldn't have mattered," Ollie pointed out with an affectionate smile for their spouse. "Nowhere is safe when Annie has a hammer."

Annie snatched her hand out of Ollie's in obviously fake displeasure. "You know, divorce is always an option."

"And who would bring you breakfast in bed every morning?"

"Every morning?" Kate asked.

"I'm spoiled," said Annie.

"No less than you deserve," said Ollie.

"Ew, stop," said Danny.

The gentle ribbing and clear affection in Jen's circle of friends enveloped Kate and Cam easily, and there was none of the awkwardness Kate had feared. When the grill made an appearance, Cam made a show of helping Ollie, mostly, Kate suspected, so that they could flex in their tight button-up to impress Danny. It seemed to be working, too. Danny stood beside them buttering buns, hip just brushing Cam's.

"Do you see what's happening here?" she whispered to Jen with a nod toward Cam and Danny.

"What's funny is I specifically told Danny not to hit on your twin," Jen said with a slight frown. Kate knocked her beer bottle against Jen's, wishing their chairs were closer together.

"I don't think it's Danny's fault. Cam has a very specific type."

"Would that type happen to be petite blond femmes?" asked Jen.

Kate waved her hand in Danny's direction. "However did you guess?"

"Is Cam single?" Jen kept her voice neutral, but Kate could see the concern in the frown still crowning her forehead.

What Jen was really asking, Kate suspected, was if it was a good idea for Danny to pursue Cam, or if Cam was bad news. She considered how her sibling presented: a sleek, cool professional with the scent of money on their clothes and a charming smile. They could be anyone.

"Cam isn't seeing anyone seriously," she said, letting Jen fill in the rest of the blanks. Cam had people they hooked up with, but nothing with commitment. "And Danny?"

"She's the best person I know."

Which wasn't what Kate had asked, but conveyed moral availability. "It isn't like we can stop them anyway. I've never had any control over Cam."

"I bet they listen to you," said Jen. "Even if they don't show it. Which of you caused the most trouble when you were younger?"

"Oh, definitely Cam. I usually went along with whatever they did to make sure they didn't get into too much trouble, but they had the bad ideas. I was the good girl."

"I bet you were," Jen said with a grin that wasn't entirely chaste. "You were a monster, weren't you?"

"Only a little." Jen winked, which tripped Kate's pulse. "You know what I'm dreading most about the next phase of the cabin?" Jen stood and held out her hand. Kate took it and rose, turning with Jen to look at the cabin, while Jen slipped her arm around Kate's waist, not pulling her close, perhaps in deference to Cam's presence, but there nonetheless. Kate leaned into the embrace.

"What?"

"Choosing curtains. My mother was obsessive about curtains. I think I have curtain trauma."

"You could always do blinds," said Kate, breathing in the now-familiar scent of Jen: cedar and iron. "Best of both worlds."

"That didn't even occur to me." Jen tilted her head as she

examined her home. "I like that. Any thoughts on color palettes, by chance?"

Laughter bubbled out of Kate, and she felt Cam's sudden attention on her. She ignored it. "I think that's something you have to decide for yourself, but yes, I do have thoughts. You should check out paint catalogs for ideas. Most have color combinations on their websites, or you can search on social media till you find design ideas you like. Though why you'd want to cover up that wood is another conversation."

"That sounds overwhelming." Jen's thumb stroked her waist. "Any chance you're available for a consult?"

Help Jen pick out her cabin color scheme? On the one hand, she'd love to. Décor was a job requirement as well as a passion. On the other, she was too aware of the impact it might leave on Jen's home if she put too much of herself into the process. Things were going well now, but there was no guarantee that would continue, and she didn't want to leave a permanent mark on Jen's life until she was sure she, herself, was permanent.

The evening was going well, Jen thought as they sat around the firepit, Kate at her side, heat pulsing pleasantly against her skin. Cam was distracted by Danny, though they were doing their best to focus on vetting Jen, and Kate seemed relaxed and happy as Ollie and Stormy regaled them with horror stories from the service industry. It was almost like every other time she'd hung out with her friends. Laughter, the smoky darkness growing around them, a distant owl—but with Kate beside her, everything seemed saturated with color.

A flicker of nerves stirred in her belly. Kate was someone she could fall for. Easily. Yes, she was gorgeous. Jen had eyes, but the calm self-assurance in the way Kate carried herself and the way she came to life when talking about the things that mattered to her were more dangerous by far.

"Hi."

Jen blinked, realizing Kate had caught her staring. She tried to cover with, "Are you warm enough?"

"You already loaned me a blanket," Kate reminded her.

"Looks nice on you." The green-and-black wool blanket wrapped around Kate's shoulders did look nice on her because anything would have looked nice on Kate.

Jesus. She'd maybe had one too many beers. She was getting sappy, and if she wasn't careful she'd say something like that aloud.

"We should probably head out soon," Kate began, sending a chill breath of air down Jen's neck. "But I don't want to leave. It's so peaceful here. You can barely hear Route 27."

"I like having you here."

She hoped that wasn't over the top. She wanted to break her own rules and ask Kate to stay the night, but Kate and Cam had driven here in the same car, which suggested Kate intended to leave with her sibling. Jen could always drive her home later if Kate wanted to stay for another drink, except there was no way Jen would drive after a few of Ollie's beers, especially if there was someone else in the car. If Kate stayed, she'd be staying the night.

Fuck, but Jen wanted Kate to stay. She looked hauntingly beautiful in the firelight, with darkness curling around her and the warm glow of the flames searing her cheeks with ruddy color. She didn't even want to touch her; just having her presence would be enough. Okay, yes, she also wanted to touch Kate. There was that. But this feeling in Jen's limbs, this yearning, needed a home.

Jen didn't sleep with people lightly, however. She'd gotten that out of her system years ago. For her to invite Kate into her bed would be taking a large next step, and she needed to be sure Kate was on the same page before that happened. She visualized splashing cold water on her face in the hopes it might sober her up a little.

"I'll walk you to your car," Jen offered.

"In a minute." Kate closed her eyes and smiled. Jen's hand

rested on Kate's armrest, their fingers interlocking. An owl called in the darkness.

"Barred owl," Jen said quietly. She knew most of the owl calls by now. How incredible would it be to sit like this with Kate every night, listening to the sounds of the forest while the moon rose over the trees?

I like you, Jen thought. *I like you too much.*

"You know, I almost didn't go to that speed dating thing," Kate said, opening her eyes to watch Jen. "I'd had a long day, and I nearly chickened out at the last minute."

"I'm glad you didn't."

"Me too." Kate teased Jen's palm with her thumbnail, which sent a wave of longing over Jen's skin. "Would you have gone out with anyone else from the event?"

"No," Jen answered. It was true.

"Not even that one woman? Blonde, pretty, seemed interested …"

"She was nice enough, but no," said Jen, wondering if Kate had felt the same stab of jealousy that Jen had felt about Kate's other dates.

"Why me then?"

Jen laughed. "Do you even need to ask?"

"I'm curious." Kate's tone was almost innocent.

"I liked your energy." And so much more, but Jen wasn't about to wax rhapsodic on the off-chance she scared Kate away. "And you know you're gorgeous."

Kate ignored the statement, but her lips twitched in a suppressed smile. "What about my energy?"

"Are you fishing for compliments?"

"Maybe." Kate's smile turned coy. It was the first time Jen had seen her lips quirk in that particular expression, and her chest tightened, as did the muscles in her abdomen.

"You're confident. You walked in like you knew we were all watching and didn't care, and you're compassionate, and funny, and just … calm, I guess? I'm not explaining it well."

"Well, that's ironic."

"Oh yeah?"

"I didn't feel calm."

"How did you feel?"

"Honestly?" Kate turned her head to give Jen the full view of her face. "Fine, till I saw you."

"And then?"

"Like the universe was playing with me."

Jen hadn't expected that. "What do you mean?"

Kate's voice grew even softer, and darkness wrapped around the fire. "You know how sometimes you see someone and you just know? Not love at first sight. I'm not trying to freak you out, but that instant connection."

Jen knew the feeling intimately. She'd felt it the minute Kate walked through the brewery door.

"Yeah?"

"Yeah." Kate dropped her eyes. "I saw you, and suddenly things became real in a way they haven't in … a very long time. Honestly? It scared me."

"I scared you?" That was unacceptable. Kate should never have to feel scared, especially for something Jen had done.

"Yeah. I like you." Kate said it simply and without hedging, a straightforwardness that rooted Jen to her chair. Kate liked her. That was definitely something. Her chest felt like it could hold the sky. "And that means I can get hurt."

"I would never," Jen began, but then she stopped herself. "Nobody can make that promise, but I would never hurt you intentionally."

"I know."

She wanted to be holding Kate right now instead of sitting beside her. There was something strangely intimate about having this conversation in the midst of a group of people, none of whom were paying them any heed. Oddly, it made her feel braver than she might have been otherwise.

"Guess we're both in the shit then," she said, the night breeze a cooling whisper on her cheek. "But sometimes it's worth the risk."

"Are you saying you're worth the risk?" The question was asked playfully, but Kate's eyes glittered.

Jen answered honestly, that foolish bravery holding the reins. "I know you are."

Chapter Seven

Kate met Cam a week later at an open house for a small Georgian-style townhome not far from Cam's work. The seller was asking too much, but that was often the case, and the days of cash offers above the asking price were nearly over.

"Try to keep an open mind," she told her twin as they neared the listing. "It's move-in ready, and while the kitchen is a little outdated, that's something you can fix down the line."

"Buying is such a commitment," Cam began.

"What's wrong with commitment?" Kate knew exactly how her twin felt about commitment, but she liked to make Cam spell out their phobia in the hopes it helped them see how ridiculous they could sometimes be. "You're committed to your job."

"I could find a different firm if I wanted."

"You can sell a house, too, you know. It's just a little more complicated."

"The maintenance, though—"

"You're such a whiner. You can learn some basic home ownership skills. It might even be good for you." She slapped Cam's thigh lightly. "Someday you're going to meet someone you want to keep around, and competence is sexy."

"You'd know," Cam said with a sly grin. "Heard from Jen?"

"We text." They texted quite a bit actually, often silly things about their days, occasionally messages with more heat.

"I like her for you."

"Really?" Kate didn't try to cover up how much she needed to hear that. Her twin's opinion carried more weight than anyone else's. She tried not to think about how few other people were in her life these days. Her new circle of burgeoning friends were Jen's, which set her up for the same risk as had happened with Morgan, but how else was she supposed to meet other queer people? Besides—Ollie was Stormy's friend, as well as Jen's, and Kate had known Stormy for years.

Still, she couldn't confide in anyone like she could Cam.

"She seems chill." Cam paused. "And I haven't heard you laugh like that in a long time."

Kate looked down at her lap, biting back a smile. "It's so hard to tell, you know?"

"That's why I don't date seriously."

"That's not why, but I'll give you a pass," said Kate. "After Morgan, I …"

Cam waited patiently for Kate to gather her words, hitting the turn signal as they approached the correct street.

"I don't want to go through that again. I want to get it right this time."

A warm hand took hers. "You'll find it."

"When, though?" She let her head rest against the seat and closed her eyes, picturing Jen's smile.

"You think it's her, don't you?"

That was the problem with someone who'd known you since conception. Cam always pinpointed any issue Kate tried talking around.

"I don't know. I like her a lot." Only a few dates in and she was falling. There wasn't much time left to withdraw without pain.

"No shit."

Kate didn't have to look at Cam to imagine their grin. "Don't be rude."

Cam scoffed at her half-hearted scolding, then asked, "Is this it?"

An open house sign stood on the small patch of lawn outside the Georgian building. Kate admired the trim on the gables and noted a pride flag hanging in a window in the house next door. Several other cars were parked along the street, more than could be accounted for in the middle of the day, which meant the open house might be bustling. That wasn't great news, but an active open house didn't always translate to offers.

"Oh no," she muttered as she recognized one of the cars, a large SUV with excessively shiny rims. She had seen the owner buffing them on several occasions.

"Hmm?"

"Todd." Todd worked for the same real estate office as Kate, and that was where the list of things they had in common ended. Todd was bombastic, egotistical and, worse, convinced that Kate would one day see the error of her ways and accept his offers of a drink after work, swooning beneath the onslaught of his masculine charm. Kate would rather drink bleach.

"Want me to deal with him for you?" Cam got out of the car and glared at the house, already gearing up for a fight.

"I have him under control. He's merely irritating."

"He pushes your boundaries," Cam corrected. "That's more than irritating. You still have that pepper spray I got you, right?"

Kate waved her keychain in Cam's face. The slim cannister of mace clinked against her keys.

"Good. People suck."

With that, they headed inside.

The listing agent had done a decent job of staging the rooms despite the current occupant's possessions. Personal photographs were all put away, along with anything that might suggest person- ality or culture. Buyers wanted to imagine themselves, not other people, in a space. Kate knew the agent by reputation. Hannah was easy to work with but pushed for fair deals for her clients. She stood off to the side of the kitchen, answering the questions of a young couple. Kate nodded in recognition and turned to Cam, only to be interrupted by a, "Kate, we have to stop meeting like this."

"Todd, what a surprise," she said, wondering if the couple with the listing agent were there with him, which would explain why he was floating about freely. "This is my sibling, Cameron."

"Pleasure to meet you." Todd stuck out his hand, forcing Cam to shake it or risk rudeness. Kate could tell Cam was tempted to do the latter, but had acquiesced for her sake. "Your sister and I go way back."

"Four years," corrected Kate. Hardly *way back* by any standard.

"You looking to buy?"

Kate let Todd engage Cam in conversation while she studied the house. High ceilings, which Cam liked. Bright windows. The floors had been redone recently, perhaps in preparation for selling, and glowed beneath the overhead lighting. She tried not to drool over the crown molding.

"…hate to be in competition." This last was addressed to her, and she snapped her attention back to Todd as he gave her what she guessed he considered a charming smile.

"Are your clients interested?"

"Very, but we'll see."

"Well, I should show Cam around." She took Cam by the arm and steered them away from Todd before they could say anything rude.

"The problem with him," she said when they'd sequestered themselves in one of the two bedrooms, "is that he doesn't ever say anything outwardly offensive. It's just the *way* he says it."

"He's a dick, Kate."

"I know that."

"He steals listings from you."

"Cam—"

"I'm just saying," said Cam.

"What do you think of the house?"

"I think it smells like Todd."

"Seriously."

"Seriously, his cologne. I dunno. It's nice, I guess. No walk-in closet, though."

"The fact that your last place *had* a walk-in is insane to me." Kate shook her head at Cam and led them through the rest of the townhome, pointing out its better attributes and giving Cam her opinion on what needed to be updated or checked in the inspection. It was almost fun—or rather, it would have been fun if she hadn't felt Todd's eyes on her most of the time. Cam was right. He was a dick, and if she was honest with herself, she hated working for the same small agency as he did. Every time she went into the office her stomach tensed in anticipation of another uncomfortable encounter. And yes—he had poached listings from her before, and then had the gall to hit on her, as if she were too stupid to realize what he'd done.

Why did everything have to always be halfway to perfect? Couldn't something in her life, for once, fulfill her hopes?

A few weeks shouldn't have been long enough to miss a person she'd only hung out with a handful of times, but there Jen was, missing Kate anyway. The upside to this state of affairs was that she'd finished putting up the wallboards downstairs, and the cabin glowed with the warmth of the pine. Jen tried to take comfort in the work. She hadn't been able to coordinate more than a cup of coffee with Kate since her small get-together. She didn't think it was intentional. Kate didn't strike her as the sort to lead her along, but then again, how well did she really know the woman?

Her phone rang. She jumped, fumbling in her work pants for her cell before remembering she'd left it on her makeshift workbench. It could be a potential client, but also—

"Hello?"

"Hi," said Kate, and with that one syllable the tension in Jen's chest melted. "I know, who calls anymore, right?"

"Realtors." Jen leaned against one of her new walls and smiled into the phone. "What are you up to? Not another flat tire?"

"I was actually wondering if you'd want to come over for a glass of wine."

"Tonight?" Jen considered the sweaty mess she'd made of herself and the time—seven thirty.

"Is it too late?"

"No, I can be there whenever you want. I just need to clean up. Text me your address?"

Which is how she found herself on Kate's doorstep with a bottle of wine she'd picked up in a hurry, her hair still damp, and nerves once more coiling her stomach into knots. Being calm and dependable was kind of her gig, and the way her central nervous system was now wreaking havoc on her sanity was unsettling, to say the least. Not that she truly minded. She didn't want to fuck this up. Kate felt right. Too right. Her friends liked her, Jen liked Kate's sibling, and the chemistry—she couldn't think about the chemistry without her body warming. Now, Kate had invited Jen into her home. This was a next step. A big next step.

Kate lived in a split-level colonial on the edge of town with a neat yard and flowerboxes bristling with mums decorating the lower windows. The house had a self-satisfied look, as if it knew the standards required of a coastal tourist town and knew, also, that it had met them. Something about it didn't quite feel like Kate. She knocked on the door to the upper apartment and tried not to swallow her tongue.

Footsteps sounded on the stairs, and then the door opened, revealing Kate in a loose pair of wide-legged pants and a slouchy sweater that made Jen want to fold her into an embrace. Instead, she proffered the bottle of wine with the chagrined smile of a guest instructed to arrive empty-handed.

"You had a Cab the other night at dinner, so I went with that. I can't promise it's any—"

Taking the bottle, Kate leaned in and brushed Jen's lips with hers, cutting off Jen's explanation. The kiss ended too soon. Jen had barely tasted her before Kate was pulling back, smiling, and offering a hand to lead Jen up the stairs and into her apartment.

It's so easy to turn your brain off, she imagined Danny saying, and then she stopped thinking about anything other than the line of Kate's shoulders as she followed her up the stairs.

"I'm sorry for inviting you over last minute," Kate said as she shut the door behind Jen and set the bottle onto the clean kitchen countertop, though Jen was relieved to see a pile of mail cluttering one end and a dish by the sink. Antiseptically clean spaces made her nervous.

"Really, no apology needed." Jen stood by the counter and watched Kate pull down two wineglasses, the sweater riding up past her hips to reveal a sudden flash of fair skin. She'd need to be on her best behavior tonight because it would be far too easy to let one thing lead to another. She wasn't ready to take Kate to bed yet.

Fuck it. Yes she was. She just wasn't ready for the emotional turmoil that would ensue afterwards if things didn't work out. Her policy toward sex was entirely defensive. She grew attached too easily, too quickly. That didn't change the slow smolder of desire building as Kate approached her with a glass.

"Come sit?"

Jen sat at the opposite end of a small couch in Kate's living room, which featured several healthy potted plants, a substantial bookshelf and, more importantly, Kate.

"I'm glad you called," said Jen.

"I had an annoying day, and as I was driving home, I realized ... well, it's been a few days, and ..."

"I missed you, too."

Kate hid a smile behind her glass. "Is that ridiculous?"

"Only if you think so," said Jen. Something moved out of the corner of her eye. A massive orange cat with a ragged ear and impressive ruff sauntered out of another room, fixing Jen with a golden gaze. It reminded her of the stray who'd been dumped at

Mary's farm. "That's some cat."

Kate laughed. "Rufus. He's a terror."

"Not too shy, either."

"He thinks he's a lion." Affection filled Kate's voice, and she wiggled her fingers toward the cat. His tail twitched, and then he trotted over and leapt up to sit on her lap, still staring at Jen with a proprietary air.

"How much does he weigh?"

"Twenty pounds of diabetes," said Kate, chucking the cat beneath his grizzled chin. "I found him scrounging in the dumpster behind the office a few years ago."

"Lucky cat." Kate's fingernails scratched Rufus's head lightly, and Jen's scalp tingled as she imagined what it might feel like to have Kate run those same nails through her hair. She'd noted on previous occasions that Kate kept her nails manicured but short, and the slight shine of the polish caught the soft light of the apartment lamps. Jen's own nails were as clean as she could get them, if a little ragged. There wasn't much point in trying to take care of them. Her hands were tools, and the work they did was rough and dirty. She appreciated the effort Kate put into her appearance, however. Manicures cost time and money. Did she do it for herself, or for her clients?

She dragged her gaze from Kate's hands to her face, finding her watching with an amused half smile. The air between them was thick with pleasant tension. Did Kate expect her to spend the night? Should she state her boundaries now, as she had before, or play it by ear?

"I like your friends," Kate said before Jen could come to a conclusion.

"They liked you." A little too much, perhaps. Ollie kept texting her for updates, which requests probably came from Annie, and Danny wiggled her eyebrows far too often these days. They were going to get stuck like that, and it would serve her right.

"It's something I didn't expect about adulthood, you know?

How hard it is to make good friends, especially queer ones." There was a wistful note to Kate's voice that tightened Jen's chest. The idea of Kate being lonely twisted inside her, barbs snaking up her throat.

"You moved here, right?"

"Yeah." Kate's wistful tone shifted to something less definable. "For my fiancé, actually. I'm from Portland originally, but after I met Morgan, we moved in together here."

"So when you broke up, you lost your community," said Jen, understanding. "That's hard, man."

"It wasn't great." Kate laughed a little, still stroking Rufus. Gooseflesh rose along Jen's arms as the cat purred. "I kept some of our friends, especially Stormy, but the rest have known Morgan for so long that it felt awkward."

"You're welcome to my friends."

Kate's smile turned wistful once more. "Thank you. I mean that. But if—I don't want to sound presumptuous—if something happens, if we don't work out, then I'm in the same boat."

If we don't work out. A mutual fear, of course, but hearing Kate stumble over the words revealed her yearning for connection. Kate *wanted* things to work.

"You can keep Ollie and Annie."

"Oh?"

"They get it. Danny . . . realistically she turns into a pit viper when people hurt her friends, so . . ." Jen tried to laugh off the comment, but Kate's gaze sharpened.

"You think I'll hurt you?"

"I think you could wreck me if I'm being honest." Jen held Kate's eyes despite the urge to look away, the rawness of her confession lying between them. In an effort to save herself, she added, "But that's the risk, right?"

"It is." Kate was still studying her thoughtfully. "Should we talk about where this is going? Or is that too much too soon? I don't want to rush—"

"We can talk about it," Jen said as Kate began speaking more quickly.

"Okay." Kate bit her lip, hands stilling on Rufus, who twitched his fluffy tail in annoyance. "I want to be honest with you."

Never a good sign. "I appreciate honesty."

"I'm not looking for something casual." She'd said as much before, though less directly. Nerves sang through Jen's blood.

"Neither am I."

"It's just that I want something real, you know? And it's so hard—" Kate broke off, perhaps absorbing Jen's reply, because she asked, "Really?"

"Really. I get attached too easily." Jen tried to make the words sound nonchalant and missed the mark. "I mean, I've tried dating casually, and it never felt right."

"Exactly. It's not that it's a waste of time, but ..."

"It's kind of a waste of time," said Jen.

Kate laughed in surprise. "I didn't want to sound like an ass."

"Yet we both attended a speed dating event."

"You have to meet people if you're going to find someone," Kate said, sounding like she was quoting something she'd been told several times.

"So I guess what we're saying is that we're on the same page?" Jen sipped her wine to hide the twitching muscle in her jaw. She'd never been particularly good at these conversations. She was too blunt. Too open. It scared people.

"I guess so." Kate took a short, nervous breath before continuing. "I could see myself falling for you, and that's terrifying."

Heat seared Jen's skin, as hot as if she stood near the forge. *I could see myself falling for you.* Should she tell Kate that she was already falling? Jen reached across the couch, grateful it was small, and cupped Kate's knee. Rufus glared in indignation.

"I know," was all she managed. "I mean, I get it. You terrify me."

As she'd hoped, Kate laughed again. "Me?"

"Are you kidding me? You're gorgeous, accomplished, can

change a tire in heels and a dress; you're kind, smart—"

Kate held up a hand to stop her, further insulting Rufus's dignity. "You're going to make me turn the color of this wine."

Jen grinned. "That's not an incentive to stop."

Kate did blush then, and Jen's stomach tightened. The flush along Kate's cheeks brought out the brightness of her eyes and the warm hue of her lips.

"Well, have you met yourself?" Kate smiled that slow, coy smile that had thrown Jen once before. She felt herself leaning forward to get closer to it. Jen suspected, too, that red wine would taste exquisite on Kate's lips.

"You're so exactly my type." Kate's self-deprecating tone didn't lessen the effect the words had on Jen. This was the second time Kate had made this comment. This time, Jen wanted clarification.

"What's your type?"

"Hot butch horsewomen, apparently." Kate's nails traced the back of Jen's hand, the light touch enough to slam Jen's eyes shut. She opened them again, hoping it would pass for a long blink, but Kate had that knowing look in her eyes, and she didn't stop drawing spirals over Jen's skin. Jen swallowed. Coals glowed when stoked, and she felt just as flammable, like the slightest breath of air might set her alight. Kate couldn't know the full extent of the effect she had on Jen, but Jen liked that Kate knew what she was doing. She liked it way too much.

"Can't say I have met my type." Her voice had a rasp to it she couldn't clear. Nor, apparently, could she form a sentence with Kate touching her.

"And what's your type?" Kate asked.

"You." No hiding the rasp at all. The word was scored with longing, the deep grooves in the single syllable giving her away.

"Lonely real estate agents?" Kate teased.

"You don't have to be lonely." Too genuine, too much, but Kate's eyes softened.

"You're sweet."

"Is that a bad thing?"

"Not at all. Come here." Kate stopped stroking Jen's hand, which was devastating, but then she gently shoved Rufus off her lap and leaned back, inviting Jen in. Jen set down her wine. Kate reclined on the couch, her hair falling over the arm. Her chest rose and fell rapidly despite the aura of control in her motions. Fuck it. Jen could restrain herself, but only to a point.

Jen braced herself above Kate and ran her fingers through Kate's hair, unable to resist. The soft strands whispered beneath her touch. Kate's eyes closed as Jen's fingers trailed down to rest on her sternum, feeling Kate's heart race beneath. Her own pulse was a perfect match, and she knew she was breathing quickly but didn't bother trying to hide it. When she pressed her hand flat over Kate's breastbone, Kate hooked her fingers in Jen's belt and yanked her close.

Arousal raced through her in a blazing torrent. This woman was going to destroy her. The press of Kate's body against hers stopped her breathing entirely, and then she was kissing Kate's neck, tasting her skin and the tensing of tendon beneath. She was so damn soft. Kate looped an arm around Jen's shoulders, her other arm trapped between them now, Kate's fingers still maddeningly curled around the top of her jeans. When Kate's nails dug into her back, Jen knew she was in real trouble. She wanted to give Kate everything—pleasure, her own body, whatever she needed.

Jen kissed along Kate's jaw, nipping the fine line of bone. Kate's back arched in response. Jen groaned, filing away each little thing Kate liked for future reference. Kate's hips sought hers and she answered, even as Kate turned her head to capture Jen's mouth. She was happy to be caught. Kate did taste like wine, but also Kate, an indefinable taste she'd come to know and crave over the last few weeks.

This kiss, however, was far more intense than any previous. Jen licked deep into Kate's mouth, stroking her tongue and catching the edge of a whimper in Kate's breath. She cupped the back of Kate's neck, using her other arm to brace herself, and sank into the fire.

It had been months since she'd truly touched another person, and the feeling of Jen on top of her opened up an abyss of longing. To be held, to be wanted—she'd forgotten how good it felt. How consuming. She arched her spine, seeking more contact, more anything really, as long as it was Jen. Jen, who was on the same page about relationships. Jen, who looked at her with such intensity she half wanted to turn away even as she wanted to bask in that attention forever.

Forever. A dangerous word. But what if? What if the reason her body opened beneath Jen's touch was because Jen was *right*?

Jen was also driving her wild, her kisses hungry and controlled, though Kate sensed that control fraying, and her hips were slowly working Kate into a nearly feral state. Kate generally liked being in control of her life, but not here. Here, she wanted Jen to take her, and she no longer cared about whether it was too soon. Her apartment surrounded them with its familiar scents and sounds: the humming fridge, the lilac infuser in the hall, a faint whiff of cat. Home. Why then did home suddenly feel like it was wherever Jen's mouth landed on her body?

"Wait," she managed. Jen sat up immediately, concern flashing over her features, but Kate merely lifted off her sweater. The shirt she'd worn beneath showed a fair amount of skin. Jen looked down at her and tugged the sweater the rest of the way off, her eyes roving over Kate's body, her jaw a little slack, her lips parted, and Kate knew she'd made the right choice.

"Fuck," Jen said. "You—"

"You can touch me."

Jen swore again, then slid her hands beneath Kate's shirt, caressing her stomach and ribs and tracing her hipbones with her thumbs. Kate's head fell back. Her next breath was ragged. Jen's warm, rough palms held her gently, and then Jen's mouth was on her again, kissing the skin just above her jeans, her dark ponytail falling over one shoulder to brush Kate's hip. Kate cried out. She hadn't meant to. She was normally quiet until she knew her partner well, but the heat of Jen's tongue was too much. Jen drew lines of fire over her abdomen. Kate bucked, seeking any kind of friction, and Jen held her down with one firm hand.

Kate lost track of time. She knew only that she never wanted Jen to stop, never wanted to not feel Jen sucking on the tender skin over her ribs, which made her whole body writhe with need. Inside her chest, her heart split open. Hope spilled out. This felt so right. She trusted Jen. She trusted her body in Jen's hands, and perhaps she could also trust Jen to hold something more. She was willing to risk it, right now. She was willing to risk everything.

"May I?"

Kate opened her eyes, aware Jen had stopped and dazed by the loss of sensation, to see Jen holding the hem of her shirt. She nodded too enthusiastically for dignity, but Jen didn't seem to mind. Quite the contrary. Jen slowly pulled Kate's shirt over her head, exposing her bra, which she'd picked out in case things took this turn. Black lacework vines hid little, and the cups barely contained her breasts.

Jen stared down at her with that slack-jawed look again, only this time the hunger in her eyes was sharp.

"God," Jen said, and it sounded like a prayer.

"Take off your shirt." Kate was proud her voice shook only a little.

Jen unbuttoned her green plaid flannel and tossed it to the floor, followed by her black undershirt. Now it was Kate's turn to stare. Jen's hips curved with feminine strength, her abdominals clenched and, dear lord, softly cut. Above that extraordinary sight, her sports bra didn't hide her breasts, and the deep dip of cleavage was an invitation.

"Who even are you?" Kate asked, hardly aware she spoke. Jen's eyes flicked up to hers for a moment, and she grinned that slightly cheeky grin Kate was coming to associate with these moments. Kate stroked a line down Jen's stomach, and that grin turned into a hiss of breath. Jen's eyelids fluttered. The motion was oddly innocent—there was an honesty to it that sank its teeth into Kate's ribs where Jen's mouth had been moments before. There was nothing innocent about the way Kate ran her nails down that smooth skin, however. Jen grabbed Kate's hand and pinned it over her head, her pupils blown and wild.

"I want you so fucking badly," Jen said, her chest heaving with her shattered breath. "You have no idea. You—" Her eyes dropped to Kate's breasts again, and Kate used her free hand to pull Jen down by the back of her neck.

Lips closed over her nipple with annihilating heat. Jen covered her other breast with the hand not pinning Kate down. The lace caught on her calluses as she kneaded and tugged, her thumb teasing the nipple as her mouth toyed with the other through the sheer fabric. Kate thought she might actually die from this. Jen cursed softly under her breath in between torturously languid strokes of her tongue, Kate's nipple taut and pulsing, and Kate couldn't help herself. She slid her thigh between Jen's and pressed. Jen ground back, her response immediate and sure, and then suddenly she pulled away, leaving Kate panting and confused.

Jen passed a hand over her face and swore again.

"What's wrong?" Kate asked, concern edging into her arousal.

"If we go any further, I don't know if I can stop myself."

"I think I've made it clear I don't want you to stop," said Kate.

"It's just I have this rule. Fuck. *Fuck.*" Jen shook her head as if to clear it. "I don't—not without commitment, and it's too soon."

Was it? Kate's arousal ebbed. It didn't feel too soon to her. Had Jen not felt how right their bodies were together? Had she not felt the same consuming magnetism? How safe Kate felt in her arms?

"We don't have to do anything you're not comfortable with," she said, because that was the right thing to say.

"It's not—*fuck*."

Kate considered pointing out that instead of repeating the word *fuck* Jen could just fuck her, but that would be disrespectful. She tried to sit up and found she was shaking with want.

"You're everything I want," said Jen.

"But?" Kate prompted, for there was a *but* lurking here somewhere.

"It's too soon for me. I'm sorry. I want to, I really fucking want to."

Cold settled in Kate's gut. "It's okay," she lied. It should be okay. She would never want to push Jen into something she wasn't comfortable doing, but this felt like rejection, and her eyes stung with tears she managed to suppress.

"I'm so sorry. I didn't mean to get carried away, but god, you have no idea what you do to me."

And clearly Kate didn't. She *thought* she'd been forging a connection, but Jen must not be feeling it as strongly. "It's okay," she said again. Maybe by repeating it she could will it to be true.

"Kate—"

Kate sat up and reached for her discarded shirt. This was fine. Jen was only saying not yet. She wasn't saying no. But Kate had been ready. She'd been ready, and Jen had stopped them, and now she didn't know what to do with herself.

"You don't have to explain yourself," Kate said.

"I do." Jen took her hand, and Kate let her. "I want this with you. I just—"

"Want commitment," Kate finished. A moment ago she would have happily given that commitment. Now, she wasn't so sure.

"I don't want to fuck this up."

She was, though, Kate thought uncharitably. Irritation swept over her in place of desire. She knew it was a self-defense mechanism but couldn't help it. "No, you're right. We should slow things down."

Best to agree. Otherwise she'd be left looking spurned.

"Is that okay with you?"

The searching look in Jen's eyes almost softened her. Almost. "Of course it's okay."

Our first lie.

Maybe Kate had gotten ahead of herself. How well did she really know Jen? Was this just the first crush she'd had since Morgan, and not a sign that things were going to work out? What was more likely—that Jen was perfect for her, or that Jen was merely a hot, kind woman who'd lowered Kate's guard? The laws of probability had the answer. Best Jen had stopped them then before Kate fell any further.

"Do you want to watch a movie?" she suggested, trying for a bright smile. She could tell by Jen's wince she'd failed.

"I have an early start tomorrow. I should probably think about heading out."

"Right. I should get to bed, too."

Jen retrieved her shirt in the terrible silence that had fallen between them, both avoiding eye contact with each other. Kate burrowed back into her sweater as if that might cushion her from further blows.

No, not blows. Jen had expressed a boundary, that was all. Things could still be okay. They felt anything but. Jen hovered once she'd dressed. It was the first time Kate had seen her unsure of herself.

"Can I kiss you?" Jen asked. Kate nodded. This kiss was slow and sad, and in it she tasted Jen's apology.

"See you later?"

All Kate could summon was a nod.

Chapter Eight

Fuck, fuck, fuck. Jen rested her head against her steering wheel and breathed deeply, trying to stifle the panic climbing up her throat. She'd ruined it. She'd gone and ruined it, and now Kate would think Jen didn't want her when that was as far from the case as possible.

She rang Danny as she drove home.

"You okay?" Danny asked immediately. "It's late."

"Sorry, I—"

"Not late in a bad way, just that you don't normally call this late so I'm assuming the worst over here." Danny spoke so quickly her words ran together, and Jen almost smiled.

"You're not far off."

"So what happened?"

"I fucked things up with Kate."

"Nooooooo." Danny drew out the word, real despair in her voice. "I liked her for you, so why'd you go and do that?"

"Things were getting . . . you know . . . and I told her I wanted to wait right as . . ."

"You cock-blocked yourself?"

"It's not like that. You know how after Laura I came up with rules."

"So?"

"One of them was I don't sleep with people I'm not committed to, and it didn't feel fair to ask her to be with me in the middle of . . ."

Silence echoed on the line, followed by Danny's groan. "You're the worst. Literally. How can you be this wholesome? Why can't you go against your values like the rest of us? Are you sure you're even attracted to her?"

"Very sure."

"Okay. Let me think. How are we going to fix this …" Danny hummed as she thought. "Well, do you want to date her? Monogamously?"

"Yes."

"You could start by telling her that."

"Do you think she'll want to hear it after that? I hurt her."

"Well, no shit. No offense, but femmes aren't used to being told to slow down. Usually it's the other way around. It probably didn't even occur to her that it was a possibility, which is fucked up now that I say it out loud, but gender roles and all that."

"I never thought about it that way."

"Of course you didn't. Again, wholesome. Ugh. How are we even friends? You're gonna have to work to fix this. She'll probably need a few days to cool off, but you shouldn't leave her alone. Text her tonight and tomorrow. Reassure her that you're into her. And then *talk to her*."

"We talked a little tonight, but then …"

"Then you got distracted, I get it. I don't blame you. She is very distracting."

"If I'd told her—"

"But you didn't, and now we need to do damage control. Don't beat yourself up about it."

"Why, so you can?"

"Yes. The good news is that once she understands what's going on in that idiot brain of yours she's going to love you. You just have to keep her around long enough. Have you told her about Laura?"

"Only that we didn't want the same things."

"Tell her that you always did what Laura wanted, and it was bad for you, and now you're learning how to be better."

"Will that work?"

"If it doesn't, then it wasn't meant to be," Danny said more gently.

"Ouch."

"Do you want me to be sympathetic now? Or do you want more advice?"

"Sympathy would be nice," Jen grumbled.

"This sucks, but it's going to be okay. She's hurting and surprised."

"I should have stayed to watch a damn movie. I left. Why did I leave?"

"She asked you to stay and you left?" Danny's voice rose with the sentence, ending with a squeak of outrage.

"I panicked."

"No shit. Okay, this is worse than I realized. You're gonna have to pull a rom-com move."

"What?"

"A grand gesture. Something that keeps her interested while you explain yourself."

"Grand gestures are stupid," said Jen. "People should talk to each other."

"No offense, but if you want to talk to her, you're going to have to show her you're invested. So. What can you do?"

"I don't know!"

"We'll think of something." Danny paused. "It really is going to be okay."

"Is it?"

"Yes. I promise." A pause filled the line. "Is this a bad time to mention I'm getting dinner with her sibling?"

Jen texted Kate the next day, but instead of bringing her a wave of excitement, Kate was awash with confusion. She considered talking to Cam about it, but couldn't bring herself to air out the wound just yet. It was too fresh. Instead, she did some paperwork and followed up with clients, Rufus on her lap, trying not to think about how Jen had been in this space only the night before. The worst part was she couldn't even be mad at Jen. Her request had been perfectly reasonable. Boundaries were healthy. It was okay to say no. She believed strongly in consent, for fuck's sake. It hardly even qualified as a rejection. Yet she couldn't help how it made her feel.

Her day did not improve when she arrived at the office. Todd's car was parked out front. She almost drove away again, but no doubt they'd already spotted her car from the office window, and, besides, she needed to make copies for an upcoming open house.

"Well, hello you," said the office manager, Denise, smiling from the desk at the front. Todd, who'd been chatting with Denise, turned to see who had come in.

"We were just talking about you," he said.

Never a good sign. "Oh?"

"Only good things."

Kate met Denise's eye for confirmation. Denise nodded. "Your sales look great this month. You're in the lead."

Well, that was something at least.

"We should celebrate," said Todd. "Have you had lunch yet?"

She hadn't, but she certainly didn't want to have lunch with Todd, even with Denise there. It would only encourage his inde-fatigable belief that women, even lesbians, found him irresistible.

"I ate, but you should go ahead and order something. Weren't you talking about that Thai place the other day, Denise?"

"I was! Are you sure we can't tempt you?"

Kate hesitated. She liked Denise. Why should Todd get to affect their relationship? It wasn't like she could afford to lose friends.

You can have mine, Jen had said. Someone else's friends could never really be your friends, though, could they? Jen, who had kissed her senseless before pulling the emergency brake.

"I suppose I could have a light lunch," she conceded.

Denise beamed. "Oh good. It gets so quiet in here, I like having you both around."

Loneliness was everywhere it seemed.

Thirty minutes later they sat around the break room table with fragrant takeout boxes piled between them. Todd chose to sit next to her instead of Denise, moving his chair too close and brushing her arm with his when he reached for his food. She leaned away.

"I was telling Todd before you got here about the vacation Steve and I are planning," Denise began, and Kate settled in for a long story, complete with photos, which at least meant she had an excuse to continue leaning away from Todd.

Unfortunately, that excuse didn't last, and when she left the office a little while later Todd followed, placing himself between her and her car door with a smug smile.

"Let me take you out for a drink," he said. "As congratulations."

"It's a little early, isn't it?"

"It's never too early to celebrate success. Come on. One drink won't kill you."

She might kill *him*, though. In fact, she'd had enough of his wheedling, and more than enough of his pathetic attempts to get her alone.

"I'm not interested, Todd." His head snapped back as if she'd slapped him. Shit. She still had to work with the guy. Time to backpedal. "I'm sorry; it's been a rough few days."

"All the more reason to knock a few back. You need to relax, Kovaleski."

Why did she even bother feeling guilty about this man?

"I'm relaxed."

He raised his brows. "Sure."

"Maybe some other time."

"Always some other time. Come on, Kate. We don't have to pretend we don't see what's going on here." His smug smile deepened. "You're single, I'm single—"

"You have a wife."

"We have an arrangement. She doesn't mind."

Kate doubted this, but it was beside the point. "I'm gay, Todd."

He leaned in to whisper, "Have you tried?"

The absolute nerve. "Have I tried men? No, I haven't."

"Then how can you really know?"

Was he for real? The things coming out of his mouth were so textbook he might have studied the *How to Be a Douche* playbook. "Have you tried?" If only slapping him wouldn't risk an assault charge. Could she argue self-defense?

"How do you know you're straight?"

"Men are different," he said with the confidence of a mediocre white man. "Women are on a spectrum."

Now he was lecturing her about sexuality?

"I'm not doing this with you."

"Just one drink. I promise you'll have fun."

"*Todd.* This is borderline sexual harassment."

"What?" He blinked. "Are you really pulling that card?"

"It's not a card. It's a fact. I said no."

"And I'm asking you to give me a chance. There's no harm in that."

Did he really believe that? Did he really have no idea of the harm that could come from this kind of pressure? No, Kate hadn't tried men, if by "try" he meant seeking one out, but she'd grown up female-bodied in a society that still valued women primarily for their bodies, and she knew the dangers the world could inflict—intimately. No, she'd never tried men, but men had been trying her for her whole damn life.

"There is, though. Plus, we work together."

He scoffed. "We see each other at the office occasionally, but we each have our own clients. I'm a good guy, Kate. Let me show you. Denise thinks we'd be cute. Her words."

Kate took a deep breath to avoid screaming. She'd have to have a chat with Denise about feeding Todd's infantile fantasy, if he was even telling the truth, which was doubtful. More likely he'd twisted what he'd heard to his liking.

"Boundaries, Todd. Please step away from my car."

"Kate—"

"I will bring this up to HR." She felt his energy shift from predatory to defensive right on cue.

"I didn't do anything. Jesus, you're all the same." His smug smile was gone now, replaced by a condescending sneer. He did move away from her door, though, and she opened and slammed it shut on his parting words, rage deafening her to whatever he'd found to throw at her from the dredges of his shallow mind.

"Call Cam," she told her phone, and the car picked up the call.

"Hey," said Cam, sounding distracted.

"Whatever you're doing, I need you to stop and listen to me before I commit manslaughter."

"What happened?"

"Fucking Todd."

She vented the entirety of her short ride home, and continued her tirade as she marched up the stairs to her apartment, tossing her stack of photocopies on the counter, where they promptly scattered, forcing her to bend and pick them up. Her hands shook with rage.

"Pour yourself a glass of wine. Do you need me to come over?" Cam asked.

"I don't know. Maybe. No. I don't know."

"I have a client dinner, but after that—"

"No, I'll be fine. Just talk me off this ledge?"

"You know I could ruin his life for you, right?" Cam sounded far too eager about that prospect.

"Motive points to me, though."

"Not when I'm done with him. That's some major creep energy. You have—"

"I have the pepper spray."

"Don't be afraid to use it on him. I'm serious. Men can be dangerous when they're humiliated."

"Don't I know it." She poured the glass of wine, splashing some over the counter and onto her cream-colored pants. "Fuck."

"What now?"

"I spilled wine on my pants."

"Laundry right now and you should be okay. Take a deep breath, though. With me. In, one two three. Out, one two three."

She breathed with her sibling. It helped marginally. Then she stripped out of her pants and carried them—and the wineglass—to the laundry room, taking a large sip as she cradled the phone awkwardly against her ear.

"Should I go to HR?"

"Hell yeah. He doesn't get to talk to you like that."

"It's going to make things uncomfortable."

"Worse than it already is?" Cam asked the question with the tone of someone who already knew the answer, so she didn't reply. "File a report, at least."

"I will."

"And I'll see what I can do."

"Cam . . ."

"What? The less you know the better. Hey, how are things with Jen?"

She suspected Cam had asked the question to try to cheer her up with a change of subject. Unfortunately for Cam, this had the opposite result. She burst into tears in her laundry room, standing in her underwear with a glass of wine, listening to Cam telling her to breathe all over again.

"It sounds so stupid," she finally managed. "We were, you know, and then she stopped and asked if we could slow down, and I don't think I handled it well, and then she left and I haven't seen her since."

"She asked you to slow down?" The protective edge was back in Cam's voice.

"Not me specifically, but us. She has this thing about not sleeping with someone she isn't in a relationship with, which I didn't know, but . . ."

"Got it. You were about to fuck and she stopped you."

"Essentially, yes. And I know it's fine, and actually cool that she has boundaries, but I asked her to stay to watch a movie and she left."

"Probably to get herself off."

"*Cam.*"

"I'm just saying it might not be for the reasons you're thinking. Maybe she got freaked out by how easily she was carried away or something. That's happened to me."

"Has it? When?"

"We're talking about you."

She accepted the evasion for now and went rooting for a pair of sweats. "So you're saying I'm the asshole?"

"No, I'm saying it's hard to react rationally in that situation. Have you talked to her since?"

"We've texted."

"When are you seeing her again?"

"I don't know. I was going to let her make that call." She found her softest, least flattering pair of sweatpants and wriggled into them, then wandered back into the kitchen, where she felt a gust of cold air and realized with a plummeting stomach that she'd left the door at the base of the landing ajar.

"Oh shit."

"Kate?"

"I can't—I left the door open. Rufus. I have to find my cat. I'll call you back."

"*Kate*—" Cam said, but she hung up and called for her boy, searching the apartment room by room. Nothing. She checked beneath the bed, in her closet drawers, behind the toilet, and all his other favorite hiding places. Nothing. She shook his canister of treats. Nothing. Panic flared at the edges of her vision. She ran downstairs in her socks and burst out into the dark of the evening, calling his name over and over.

"Rufus!" She'd forgotten a flashlight. Shit. She ran back upstairs and grabbed her phone, then ran back down, ignoring a missed call from Cam. Maybe he was hiding in the bushes? She shined the light into the evergreens, parting them to peer into the depths. Nothing. Cam called again.

"What?"

"You're freaking out. He'll come back when he's hungry."

"He has diabetes, Cam. If he gets lost, he'll be dead in four days. Maybe sooner. He needs to eat, or else he'll get hepatic lipidosis—"

"What?"

"It's a veterinary thing. He could *die*, Cam." Her voice cracked, and tears flowed down her cheeks once more.

"I'll be there in forty-five."

"No, you can't cancel your dinner."

"I can. Done."

"Cam—"

"Go look for him. I'll be there soon." Cam hung up, leaving Kate in the garden with the wind picking up. She searched the backyard, small as it was, and shone her light into her neighbors' gardens, calling his name until her voice grew hoarse.

Her phone rang again.

"I can't find him," she said, not bothering to check caller ID. "Who?"

"What?" She held the phone out to see the ID and almost cried again. Of course. Jen. "Sorry, I thought you were Cam. My cat got out and I can't find him and I'm freaking out."

"I'll be right there."

"You don't need—"

"He has diabetes, right?" Jen asked, and Kate heard the sound of keys jingling in the background and the click of a door shutting. "So he can't be outside for long."

Kate couldn't help it. She started crying again, relieved that she didn't need to explain herself.

"Hey," Jen said in a soothing voice that probably worked on all the animals, but only made her cry harder. She wiped her eyes and nose and sniffled. "I'll be there in ten minutes, okay?"

"Okay," she managed to hiccup. Then she hung up and continued her search.

Chapter Nine

Jen parked on the street and leapt out of her truck, flashlight in hand, after driving slowly through the neighborhood looking for any sign of a fat orange cat. She saw no cats, but did see Kate, who was walking down the road in her socks with only her phone flashlight for illumination. Jen jogged to catch up and put an arm around Kate's shoulders when Kate turned to look at her from bloodshot eyes. Kate melted against her, a few sobs shaking her frame before she gathered herself and straightened. Jen selfishly wouldn't have minded if she'd stayed in her arms a little while longer.

"Where have you looked so far?"

Kate gestured at the area around her house.

"Okay. Let's go get you some shoes and a jacket, and then we'll come back and keep looking. Do you have treats or anything he might come to?"

"Yeah," said Kate, sounding very small. "What if we can't find him?"

"Then we'll put up posters and call animal control and the local vet clinic." Which meant Kate's ex, but that didn't matter right now. "We'll find him."

Kate obviously wanted to believe this, but she wasn't a fool. They might not find him, and that possibility shredded Jen's insides. No, she'd find this damn cat if it killed her. First, though, she had to take care of Kate.

Kate threw on a pair of sneakers and a wool coat, then got half-way down the stairs before she sprinted back up to grab the treats.

"He loves these."

Jen put her arm around Kate's shoulders again and held her for a moment. Kate blinked tears furiously away.

"It's been such a shitty day, and I wasn't paying attention, and I left the door open."

"It happens," said Jen, trying for her most consoling tone. "It could happen to anybody. It doesn't make you a bad pet owner."

"It does, though. I should have been more careful."

"Let's just look for him, okay?"

Kate nodded and let Jen take her hand. With their free hands, they wielded the flashlight and the treat cannister, working together to search along the street and the one behind it, peering into yards and gardens and behind trash cans and up trees. The damn cat was nowhere. Kate grew more panicked as time passed, and Jen looked harder. She would not let this woman, who had confessed to being lonely only the night before, lose her feline friend like this.

Another car pulled up beside them as they rounded the corner of the street for the third time.

"Want me to cruise the neighborhood?" asked Cam.

Kate nodded. "You didn't have to come all—"

"I told them I had a family emergency; it's not a big deal." Based on the very nice shirt and suit jacket Cam was wearing, Jen sensed this wasn't entirely true, but she respected Cam's choice. Family over work.

"We'll keep searching this area," said Jen when it became clear Kate needed someone to take charge. "He might be freaked out and hiding."

"Yeah, good point. Okay, I have my phone. I'll call if I see anything." Cam pulled away in their sleek car, the headlights illuminating the block.

Two hours later, even Kate was flagging.

"Put his food out with his meds," Jen suggested. "I can get

a trap from a friend of mine who works with ferals and bring it by tomorrow, too." Mary wouldn't mind loaning her one of her many traps.

"What if we can't find him?" Kate asked again. Jen folded her into a hug and kissed her temple. She couldn't bear the weight of Kate's despair for her, but she could hold her.

"We'll try everything before we give up. Come on."

Cam materialized with a box of pizza, and the three of them sat in Kate's living room, Cam and Jen exchanging worried glances while Kate stared at the floor.

"You should eat," Cam tried again.

"I can't."

"I know, but you should anyway." Cam offered Kate a small slice. She accepted it, but made no move to bring it to her mouth.

"He was with me through everything with Morgan, and before."

Jen's body tensed with sympathetic anguish. If she lost Mabel, how would she feel? Just as lost, no doubt, and just as distraught.

"I know," said Cam. "He's your idiot baby."

Far from offending Kate, that seemed to crack a small smile, and she nibbled on the tip of the pizza.

"At least he knows how to hunt," Cam continued. "Will that help with the lipid-whatever?"

"It might. He needs to eat, which he won't want to do if he starts feeling bad."

Jen didn't ask for clarification on the veterinary jargon. What mattered was the cat was sick and needed to be rescued. She pulled out her phone and shot a text off to Mary about borrowing a trap, apologizing for the late hour. Hopefully she was smart and had notifications silenced. Jen didn't understand people who didn't take that precaution, unless they were on call like Kate's ex. Jen could offer her that much, at least. There were no work emergencies that would wake her in the middle of the night. This wasn't the time to be thinking about how she could do better than Morgan, however. She needed to reassure Kate, yes, but first she had to help her find her cat.

"Are you okay if I take off?" Cam asked some time later, after they'd made sure Kate ate and drank and changed out of her filthy socks.

"Yeah." Kate hugged her sibling goodbye and walked them to the door, her shoulders slumped and defeated. Jen wanted—needed—to take her into her arms and hold that curve of pain, offering a bolster against the fear of loss, but she didn't rise from her spot on the couch. Kate turned once the door was shut with a question written in her brows.

Jen spoke quietly into the silence. "I can stay. I'd like to stay unless you'd rather be alone."

Kate shook her head and took a hesitating step toward the couch. The sight was devastating. Jen held open her arms, and Kate collapsed into them, curling up on the couch like a cat herself and burrowing her face into the crook of Jen's neck, her breath hot but steady. She'd cried herself out for now, it seemed. Jen stroked her back, soothing her as best she could with the comfort of another body.

They didn't speak. Kate remained curled in Jen's arms until her breathing steadied into sleep. Carefully, Jen reached for the blanket draped over the arm of the couch and spread it over Kate's shoulders, covering them both, then rested her own head against the back of the couch and closed her eyes. Contentment filled her like smoke. She almost felt guilty. It was wrong to feel this swelling happiness when Kate was heartbroken, but there it was.

Happiness. It had been so long since she'd held a woman she cared for. Years, if she was counting. The smell of Kate's hair flooded her with each inhale, and she sorted past floral notes from her shampoo to the dark, heady scent beneath.

Mabel would be fine till morning, if a little confused. Jen would leave Kate around six after making her a cup of coffee. She'd worry later about the crick this would put into her neck and back—nothing she couldn't work out with a wall and a lacrosse ball. Sacrificing her own comfort for Kate was the easiest choice she'd made all day.

Kate woke to the smell of coffee and a hand on her shoulder. She blinked, confused at first by her surroundings. She wasn't in her bedroom, and she wasn't alone.

"Cam?" she murmured, wiping sleep out of her eyes and sitting up.

"Not quite," said Jen, holding out a steaming cup of coffee.

The night came back to her in little rivulets, details piling up on each other around the bends. Rufus. Flashlights in the dark. Jen saying, *I can stay.*

She had stayed. All night. And Kate—had she fallen asleep on her? Part of her began the process of mortification, but she was too heartsick and grateful to care. Jen had stayed. Maybe it was pity, but she couldn't convince herself of that, either. Not when Jen's rich brown eyes gazed at her with such earnest concern. She accepted the cup of coffee and tried not to think about morning breath or how tousled she must look, still in her clothes from last night, though at least she was in sweats. Her least attractive pair of sweats. But, again, she couldn't bring herself to care. Rufus was missing, and Jen had stayed. Those were facts. She clung to the latter as she sipped the dark coffee, lightened a little by a splash of milk, exactly the way she liked it.

Jen had memorized how she took her coffee. The wall she'd tried to build the previous day crumbled.

"Thank you," she said, meaning not just for the coffee, but for sharing the ordeal of the night before, and for the discomfort of sleeping on a couch, and for the gentle pressure of Jen's hand on her knee as she crouched before her. The dark smudges beneath Jen's eyes no doubt matched her own.

"Of course." Jen touched Kate's cheek. "You know I'd do

anything for you, right?"

Anything except sex, the self-conscious part of her brain supplied, but she was wiser this morning.

"I'm sorry about how I reacted last night," she said, setting down her coffee. "I was caught up in the moment, and—actually there isn't a good excuse. You have the right to set your own boundaries."

"You don't need to apologize." Jen's voice was a caress. "It's on me, too. I should probably tell you about Laura."

"Your ex?"

"Yeah." Jen brushed Kate's cheek with her thumb one more time then clasped their hands together. Kate wondered if she was comfortable crouching like that but didn't want to let go of Jen's hand. "We were together for three years. She was great in her own way. Driven. Dedicated to her job. Maybe a bit like your Morgan. The problem was that I did whatever she wanted, whenever she wanted, until I'd sacrificed my own life for her career, fitting myself into what she wanted me to be. I wanted land and a family. She wanted to move to a city, and she didn't want kids, so I convinced myself I didn't either. And that worked for a while. Until she met someone else."

Kate exhaled sharply with fury. Who would cheat on Jen?

"She didn't cheat on me," Jen said, guessing Kate's thoughts. "She told me she had feelings for someone else, but that she hadn't acted on them, which was better than the alternative."

"Not by much."

"No, not by much." Jen smiled as if the memory didn't hurt. "But I was left with a life I'd built around someone else's needs and had no idea what I even wanted anymore. So I moved back home and started up my practice, reconnected with Danny and the others, and figured my shit out. One of the things I decided was that I wasn't going to compromise myself for someone else again, not unless they were willing to compromise, too. And I know—" Jen broke off here and looked down at the carpet. "If I sleep with you, Kate, I'm going to fall even harder for you than I already have, and I want that, but I need to know—"

"Willyoudateme?" Kate blurted out.

Jen's brows contracted in confusion. "I didn't quite—"

"Will you date me? Exclusively?" The words left her light-headed. She almost panicked. Was it too soon? What if they only seemed to want the same things? What if she was putting Jen in the same situation she'd been in before—or worse, herself? But Jen wanted a family, like Kate did. Work wasn't her sole focus. She was kind, and funny, and talented, and gentle, and besides—Kate had already fallen. There was only one direction she wanted this to go, and that was forward.

"You don't have to say that just because—"

"I'm not." Kate's voice firmed as she grew more confident with her decision. "I want you. I want us to work out, and I'm willing to risk it not working if that means I get to be with you. I know I'm a mess right now, but—"

Jen took her face in her hands and moved to kiss her.

"Wait," Kate said, pressing a hand against Jen's chest. "I have terrible morning breath, and coffee—"

"Kate," Jen said solemnly, "do you really think I fucking care about that right now?"

Kate didn't have time to answer before Jen surged into her, the force of the kiss pressing Kate back into the couch as Jen straddled her, hands warm on her jaw, the intensity of her response the affirmation Kate needed.

When Jen pulled away, they were both breathless. Jen ran her fingers through Kate's loose hair, raising goosebumps along Kate's arms, her eyes flickering over Kate's features.

"We'll find your boy," Jen said with a certainty Kate longed to believe. "I'll pick up that trap today and bring it by. Do you have work you have to do?"

She did, unfortunately.

"I'll take some of his cat food in case you're not home so we can catch him if he comes back while you're out."

"Will you come by later? After you finish work?" Kate asked, aware she sounded a touch desperate.

"As soon as I take care of Mabel."

"Mabel! I'm so sorry. I forgot about her. Do you have to go?" Kate briefly resented Jen's dog before scolding herself. Jen was here helping her find her cat. The least she could do was spare Jen a few moments for the sake of her dog.

"In a minute." Jen's eyes fell back to Kate's lips. "First I want to hear about why your day was shitty yesterday."

The last thing she wanted to talk about was Todd. The thought of him crawled over her skin on cold, damp paws. She also knew that keeping the experience entirely to herself could lead to scar tissue, her heart growing callused around the wound. Better to cleanse it.

"Oh." Kate swallowed. "I have this coworker, Todd, who isn't good with boundaries."

Jen's hackles rose instantly. "What kind of boundaries?"

"He's been trying to get me to go out with him for almost a year. He never says anything super offensive, well, until the other day, but he's . . ."

"A creep?" Jen supplied. Her heart was pounding with adrenaline. She'd find this guy and shove a hot poker through his chest. How dare anyone make Kate feel uncomfortable. "What did he say?"

"He asked me if I'd ever tried men, implying I couldn't be sure I was a lesbian unless I had."

"Because that's how sexuality works . . ."

"Then he told me that women's sexuality was more fluid than men's."

Jen would kill this man. Maybe not literally, but she'd give him a piece of her mind.

"He also poaches listings from me, but that's just regular shitty, not . . . this. He put himself between me and my car until I threatened to talk to HR."

Jen tried very hard to sound measured as she asked, "How did he take that?" but what she really wanted to do was go back in time and put herself between Kate and Todd. She knew that kind of posturing. Subtly aggressive, it was a reminder that Kate couldn't make him move, perhaps even with physical force, and it put her at his mercy.

"You should talk to HR," said Jen. "He shouldn't get away with shit like that."

"It isn't that big of a deal. He did move, eventually, but it pissed me off."

"It is a big deal." Jen felt heat enter her voice and tried to quench it. She wouldn't make Kate manage her reaction on top of what had already happened to her. "People like that test your boundaries to see how much they can get away with."

"I didn't let him get away with it."

"No," Jen said, ceding the point but unwilling to bend. "That's true, but you should report it in case he tries something else. Then there's a pattern of behavior on record."

"I'll think about it."

Jen wanted to push her, to make her promise she would tell HR about the slimy bastard, but it wasn't her place. Instead, she said, "I'm so sorry you have to deal with that."

"Thanks." Kate looked down at her with a sad twist of a smile. "It could be so much worse."

"Don't minimize it. He's your coworker and it sounds like he's been making you uncomfortable for a long time. That's bullshit."

"Still—"

Jen raised an eyebrow and gently squeezed Kate's calves.

"Okay, yes. It is bullshit."

"Thank you." All she wanted was to make this situation go away—Todd, the missing cat, all of it.

"I was upset by it and left the door open. That's what happened to Rufus."

"See? Bullshit."

Kate stroked Jen's jaw with a hand warmed by the mug of coffee. "Could you be less perfect?"

Jen flushed. "Perfect is a stretch. I could get you more coffee, though, once you finish that cup."

"See?" Kate sipped her coffee, hand still on Jen's jaw. "Perfect."

The damn cat didn't come back that night, nor was he in the trap the next morning. Jen spent the night with Kate again, cuddling on the couch while they played a movie to take Kate's mind off her worry, and then cuddling in Kate's bed, where Jen held her and didn't try to touch her beyond comforting her, for when they kissed, Kate's lips were salted with tears. Jen called the vet clinic and the shelter, but no one had brought in a stray cat. Animal control hadn't seen an orange cat either. Jen drove around the neighborhood looking for the worst-case scenario, but she didn't see any feline bodies on the side of the road.

So she did the only thing she could think of, and in between appointments she went door to door in Kate's neighborhood, asking if anyone had taken in a stray. Not everyone answered the door, and those who did hadn't seen a cat, though they promised to call Kate if they did.

The cat wasn't the only thing on her mind. She kept thinking about Kate's douchebag coworker, and as a result had to fight to tamp down her rage. How dare that man—how dare any person— make Kate feel uncomfortable while trying to do her job. The sheer audacity of it didn't surprise her, but she worried about what he might do next. She couldn't intervene on Kate's behalf without Kate's permission, but, despite believing in nonviolence, she longed to crush the man's nose with her fist. She'd make *him* feel like prey and see how she liked it. Nobody fucked with her girlfriend.

Girlfriend. The tumult of emotions inside her turned again,

from worry to anger to a blooming happiness that pushed out all else. Kate had asked her to be her girlfriend. Now if only she could prove good on her promise and find Kate's cat.

That afternoon she searched dumpsters behind nearby Seal Cove businesses for evidence of feline activity, though racoons left a similar calling card. This eventually brought her to Stormy's café.

"Well, this brightens my day," Stormy called out from behind the register of Storm's-a-Brewin' café and craft brewery. Jen passed through the neatly arranged café tables and hipster-chic décor and beneath glass globes of air plants and succulents till she came to the counter.

"I'll take a coffee to go, but I'm actually here about a cat. Any chance you've seen a ginger tom around?"

"Is he yours?" Stormy asked, concern tightening her generous mouth. "I haven't seen one, but I'll keep my eyes open."

"It's Kate's, actually."

"Oh." Stormy brightened. "That must be going well then if you're out here looking for her kitten."

"You could say that." She couldn't suppress her grin.

"You have excellent taste, my friend, though I know I don't have to remind you who to thank." Stormy winked. She and Ollie were incorrigible.

"You were right, as usual."

"I know." Stormy's smile had a higher wattage than most lightbulbs, and Jen couldn't help laughing.

"Not that you're a smug asshole about it."

"You love it and you love me. Oh!" Stormy brightened still further. "I have a security camera out back. It has the dumpster in view I think. I can look at footage to see if any kitty cats are out and about."

"Could you? Thanks, man."

"My genuine pleasure. Now, I have a few different beans. The Guatemalan is particularly good if I do say so myself, and I do."

"I'll try it."

"Anything for your girlfriend?" Stormy winked again.

"Actually, yeah," Jen said, an idea forming in her mind. "Your darkest roast and a splash of milk."

Chapter Ten

Kate sat in her car outside the office for a full five minutes before working up the courage to go inside because of course Todd's car was there. He was always there. Sometimes she wondered if he lay in wait for her or if he couldn't stand being alone.

"Good morning," she said, frost sparkling through her voice as her gaze swept over a scowling Todd to land on Denise. She gave her a tight, if genuine, smile.

"Morning," Denise said brightly. Her eyes did flicker toward Todd, however, proving she wasn't as oblivious as she sometimes pretended.

"I have a favor to ask." Kate turned her back to Todd and leaned on Denise's desk. "My cat got out the other day, and he hasn't come back. I was going to run a few copies of a poster, twenty tops, if that's okay with you."

"Of course! Oh, the poor baby. It's awful when they do that."

"Technically, that's theft of office supplies," Todd interjected. "Not that I'm going to narc to HR, or anything."

Subtle he was not.

"Oh hush." Denise waved him away. "It's a few cents."

"Still, we should be ethical."

"Speaking of ethics, I'd hate to think about what we'd find if we looked through all the office computers," said Kate, keeping her back turned to him, though the nape of her neck prickled as her instincts warned her that turning her back on a potential threat was a mistake.

"Everyone scrubs their search histories," Todd said dismissively.

"I don't. Do you, Denise?"

"Of course not! Nothing I need to hide."

"Well, that's interesting." Kate ignored the look of discomfort on Denise's brow. She didn't want her in the middle of this, but she also had to make her point. Blackmailing her over a few missing-cat posters wasn't going to get Todd out of a call from HR. And she *would* call HR, she decided, heart racing with fury. How dare he try to act like she was the one in the wrong.

The door jingled, and Kate kept her gaze fixed on Denise. "So, a few copies are okay?"

"Of course, honey. Print as many as you need. Can I help you?" This last was called over Kate's shoulder in Denise's cheeriest customer service voice. Kate glanced behind her, then turned around fully, her mouth stuck in an *O* of surprise.

Jen stood in the doorway, holding a cup of coffee and a pastry bag from Stormy's café, looking hot as hell in her Carhartt pants and leather jacket, hair in its usual ponytail.

"Thought you might need an extra boost," said Jen. Kate noted the way Jen's eyes flashed to Todd, but Jen didn't do anything so obvious as glare. A smile curved Kate's lips. She'd texted Jen that she was on her way to the office, lamenting the prospect of a run-in with Todd, and Jen had come to back her up.

"I do," she said, stepping toward Jen and giving her a swift, chaste kiss that nonetheless made its point.

"Denise, Todd, this is my girlfriend, Jen."

"So nice to meet you!" Denise stood and came around the desk to shake Jen's hand enthusiastically. Todd's scowl had shifted to a look of surprise, then doubt, before returning to an even deeper scowl than before.

"Todd," he said, introducing himself unnecessarily since Kate'd just done the honors, but sparing him having to say anything as polite as Denise had.

"Kate's mentioned you," said Jen. Kate stifled a smirk. Jen couldn't quite conceal the steel in her voice, or the implied threat.

"I didn't realize you had a new beau." Denise rushed to fill the awkward silence. "What do you do, Jen?"

"She's a farrier," Kate said proudly.

"Horse feet?" Todd's scoff instantly turned Kate's blood to steam.

"They're called hooves, actually," Kate said. "Not just anyone has the guts to work on thousand-pound animals."

Jen's affectionate gaze warmed as she looked at Kate, and Kate relaxed against her. She could do this. She could deal with Todd, even with Rufus missing. She had backup now. Not that she wouldn't have reported him otherwise, but it felt nice to have someone so squarely in her corner. Todd mumbled something about going to his office and beat a hasty retreat. Kate wasn't naïve enough to think he'd let things drop after this. Having the upper hand, however, boosted her resolve. She mouthed an *I'll tell you later* to Denise, who nodded before asking Jen several questions about her job.

"I should have asked Kate how you take your coffee," Jen said to Denise. "I would have picked you one up, too."

"Ooh, this one's a keeper." Denise patted Kate's arm in congratulations and gave Jen another beaming smile. "I'll let you make those copies now, but *you* are welcome to stop by any time."

"Thank you," Kate said when she'd led Jen to the back office she used. Jen shut the door and set the coffee and pastry bag on the desk.

"I know you have the situation under control, but thought you might need a palate cleanser." The glare Jen gave the door was unmistakable, and there was a tension to her body that let Kate know Jen wouldn't mind taking Todd outside for a private chat.

Kate stepped closer, running her fingers down the jacket. "This is nice on you."

"Danny ordered me to wear it when I took you out to dinner."

"Danny has good taste."

"She certainly thinks so."

Kate kissed her, stanching further conversation. Jen spun her and pinned her against the door. Todd left Kate's thoughts. Jen's kiss was possessive and hungry, and Kate melted beneath it, gripping tightly to Jen's jacket. Jen smelled like crisp fall air and horse. It was intoxicating.

Kate sought Jen's mouth when Jen broke the kiss, eyes fluttering open. Jen brushed Kate's lower lip, hunger still in her gaze. "Let's make some copies, yeah? Then you can get out of here and away from that jackass."

Jen was idling outside Kate's apartment with her car full of "missing cat" posters, hoping the landlord, who lived below, wasn't home to be freaked out by her presence when she saw the orange flash. *Fucking cat.* She keyed off the ignition and leapt out of her truck before slowing, not wanting to spook the cat and terrified she'd imagined the brief glimpse of fur. Shutting the door gently, she peered over the hood of her truck to see—

That little bastard. Rufus crept back up onto the front stoop and circled the trap, tail twitching, but didn't enter. Slowly, Jen pulled out her phone to text Kate, who was at a showing until four.

Any chance this guy's been trapped before? Because he's not buying it. He's back, though.

She put her phone away and considered her options. She didn't think Rufus would come to her if she approached him, not if the way he'd glared at her from Kate's lap was any indication. On the other hand, it had been three days since he'd gotten out. If his diabetes was acting up, shouldn't he be too sick to run? Her horse sense suggested that was just when he'd be mostly likely to run, however, and she worried her cheek between her molars. There was a reason for the expression *herding cats.* They were difficult to corral at the best of times, let alone when they were on edge and flighty. If she had a key to Jen's place, she could try opening the door and shooing him inside, but she'd have to get to the porch first without spooking him.

Fuck-muffins, as Danny liked to say.

For now she'd wait and see if he went into the trap. With luck he'd linger until Kate came home in an hour and a half. Without luck . . .she wondered how the neighbors would feel if she tore through their yards in pursuit. She hoped none had a handgun close by. Once again she considered the situation as if Rufus were a horse. Approach from the side, where the horse could see you, moving slowly but steadily. No erratic motions. Calm voice. And then . . . she grabbed him? At least she was wearing long sleeves. That might minimize the damage he could inflict upon her.

Rufus did not enter the trap. He sat for a while on the step, cleaning a front paw and not acting at all like a cat about to succumb to ketoacidosis. He seemed rather content actually, blinking in the sun, the doormat no doubt warmer beneath him than cold concrete. Her phone buzzed and she checked the message as surreptitiously as possible.

You see him?!?!?! I'll be there as soon as I can!

No answer about the trap, but Jen suspected her suspicions were right, and Rufus was wise to the ways of small metal boxes. Otherwise, why would a presumably hungry cat avoid it?

The front door of the downstairs apartment opened. Rufus fled around the house, and Jen was off after him, shouting, "It's Kate's cat," over her shoulder as an older woman with tight gray curls peeked out to stare at her.

The backyard consisted of a small stretch of lawn, a low fence, and a carefully maintained, but dying, garden. She scanned the thinly leafed shrubs and deck. Beneath the deck? She crouched. Nope. That would have been too convenient. From her position on her haunches, however, she could see into a bed of hydrangeas along the far fence line, where a pair of yellow eyes blinked at her defiantly.

"Hey buddy," she tried. "Here kitty kitty."

She hadn't expected it to work, and it didn't. He didn't run, though, which was something.

"Someone's very worried about you." The autumn air held a hint of deeper cold. They'd have a hard frost tonight, and while Rufus would be fine in healthy circumstances, she wasn't sure he'd make it in his compromised state. "It's gonna be cold tonight," she told him, keeping her voice low and calm. "You have a nice warm bed inside. Let me take you there, and I'll give you a can of tuna, too."

Or not. She'd leave that up to Kate. She wasn't sure if diabetic cats had dietary restrictions.

"Wouldn't you like some tuna?"

Rufus was not interested in tuna.

"Please, buddy?" Slowly, she stood. He twitched that expressive tail but didn't bolt. She took a cautious step toward him. "She's gonna be so happy to see you, little guy. I'll let you scratch me if that makes you feel better. I get it. Can't go down without a fight."

She continued this stream of niceties as she inched a few more feet. Three yards separated them now, but if he ran that wouldn't matter. She wished she had cat treats. All her pocket contained was stale horse biscuits, however, so that was out. Her only option was to catch him and hope his reflexes were slowed by illness.

"Who's a handsome boy?"

The handsome boy growled as she advanced another foot. *Easy,* she cautioned herself.

"Lots of big dogs around here," she tried. "I'm not as scary as they are, am I? No? You're not scared? Just pissed? I get that, I get that. I respect your choices, dude, I really do, but you can't stay outside."

His hiss said otherwise.

"I'm going to come just a little bit clo—nope, just kidding." She froze as he twitched, body coiling to spring away, and she waited until he'd settled back down. This close he didn't look as robust as she'd initially thought. Something about his eyes was off, and his fur was ragged rather than regal. "You don't feel good, do you, buddy?"

This earned her another warning growl, but she chose to think she was getting through to him and advanced four inches. Two yards. Maybe she could pull this off. She crouched and extended her hand slowly. "See? Nothing scary here. Just me. We've met. I like your mom. You like your mom. We're on the same team. Or we have the same team captain. I'm not good at metaphors. Jesus, you look really rough, bud."

It was harder to move at a crouch, but less threatening. She scuffed one boot over the grass and then the other. Five feet. He hissed again, and she froze, letting him think he had some control in the situation—because he did, when it came down to it. "Easy, Mr. Man."

Mr. Man maintained a low growl as she inched closer still, easing her hand back until she held it loosely before her, elbow bent, Rufus within reach were she to extend it. He hissed and bared his teeth, but still he didn't run. Now what? Did she lunge for him and hope she was faster, which was unlikely even in his condition, or did she try to slowly reach out and hopefully scruff him?

He moved, and, without thinking, Jen threw herself forward into the bush, closing her eyes at the last second to avoid puncturing her cornea, and blindly snatching for any bit of cat she could reach. Her hands closed over fur and she seized onto what turned out to be a hind leg, as, she opened her eyes to a very angry Rufus, turning in his own skin like a snake in a sack to attack her forearm with three sets of claws and one set of sharp teeth. Her sleeves staved off the worst of the damage, but his claws ripped the back of her hand open when she went to grab him. She gritted a curse out between her teeth and seized him by his scruff. You weren't really supposed to scruff cats, she recalled, but if ever there was a time, this was it. He continued his assault on any bit of her he could reach.

"Hey, hey, hey, buddy, cool your little jets." The only thing she could think to do now was hug him to her in the hopes of quelling his rage. To her surprise, it worked. He merely twitched in her arms, which was a vast improvement. She stood and began walking toward the trap, where she'd have to stash him until Kate got home, when a gnawing sense of wrongness caused her to look down.

"Fuck," she swore, and sprinted toward her truck.

She was halfway home when Jen called, and she knew immediately that something was wrong.

"I have him, but he's having a seizure, so I'm taking him to the vet right now."

Cold fear seeped through her pores to consume her. This had been what she was afraid of with his diabetes.

"Oh my god—"

"I have him, though. He's not outside anymore, and the clinic's only five minutes away."

"I'm on my way. Stay on the phone with me in case something happens?" Her voice broke on *something*. Not Rufus. He'd been with her for four years, her constant companion, her little orange shadow. A sob wracked her chest, but her eyes stayed dry. She was too terrified to cry.

She remembered the day she'd found him in the dumpster behind the office, rangy and handsome with his massive ruff and fluffy tail. He'd blinked at her, and she'd taken one look at his ragged ear and called Morgan, who had provided a trap and some cat food. Technically they'd gotten him together, but he had always been her boy, choosing her lap, her side of the bed, and her legs to wind between. Morgan was good for feeding him and that was about it as far as he was concerned. She secretly loved that about him, especially on the long winter nights when Morgan was called in to work and she sat alone in front of the television or with a book, pretending she wasn't lonely. Losing him wasn't an option, especially when it was her fault. He deserved better.

Jen's truck was in the small parking lot when she arrived. Kate flung herself out of her car, barely remembering to put it in park, and raced to the door, nearly tripping over a man exiting with a dachshund.

Jen sat in the waiting room without Rufus.

"Where—"

"They took him to the back," Jen said when she couldn't finish the question. "Dr. Lee took him even though they don't technically take emergencies. She thinks they can get him stabilized."

Bless Lilian Lee, Morgan's veterinary school friend, for making an exception. She sat next to Jen and tried to stop her hands from shaking. One of her legs bounced up and down out of her control. Minutes passed, then half an hour. No news was good news, right? That meant he was still alive and Dr. Lee was working on him.

"Kate?" She leapt to her feet when an exam room door opened. Lilian held the door open. Kate's feelings about losing Morgan's friends stayed dormant as she rushed inside.

"He's okay," Lilian said.

Kate burst into tears. Jen, she realized, hadn't followed her in, but Lilian squeezed her shoulder, then gave her a hug. She'd missed Lilian's hugs. A box of tissues was discreetly pushed toward her, and she took one gratefully, trying to regain some control of herself.

"I let him out by accident," she said.

"Cats are like that. They see an opening and they take it. It isn't your fault."

It was, but she didn't argue. She wanted to hear the update far more than she wanted to punish herself.

"He's on fluids for the dehydration, and I've given him some short-acting insulin to bring down his blood sugar and decrease the ketone levels, and also some potassium. He's very lucky you found him when you did. He's not critical, but it was a near thing."

Lilian didn't ask about Jen, and Kate didn't offer any explanation. What Lilian told Morgan about this was up to her, not Kate.

"When can I take him?"

"Come back at the end of the day and we'll discharge him. He's lucky to have you."

Even though I let him out? Paying for his care was the least she could do, especially since she could put it on a credit card. Not everyone had that option.

"I can't thank you enough."

"It's my pleasure, and my job. Kate . . ." Lilian trailed off.

"It's okay," Kate said.

"It's not. You know we love you. It's just . . ."

"It was too painful for her. I get it. I really do."

"It isn't fair, though."

Kate shrugged. "Most things aren't. I'm glad you were there for her."

"Maybe we could get coffee sometime?" Lilian suggested, though Kate doubted she'd follow up.

Still, she said, "I'd like that."

They chatted for another minute or two; then Lilian excused herself and Kate retreated to the waiting room and Jen.

"I wasn't sure if you'd want me coming in with you," Jen said as they walked out of the hospital together. "I'm sorry if I made the wrong call."

"It's okay. You were here. But in the future, yes, please come with me."

Jen tucked her arm around Kate's waist and gave her a reassuring squeeze. "He's okay, though?"

"For now. Thank you for catching him." Jen held Kate's car door open for her, and Kate winced. "Did he do that to you?"

"It's not a big deal."

"Have you cleaned it? Cat scratches can cause nasty infections."

"Haven't had time yet, but I will. Don't worry about it. You have other things to take care of."

"Am I not allowed to worry about you?" Kate wished, once again, that she could arch either of her eyebrows.

Jen grinned. "I wouldn't start worrying about my hands if I were you. You've seen them, right? They're all jacked up."

"They are also the tools of your trade. Scars are one thing, infection another."

"Then I promise to clean it very well, and I'll even let you monitor it."

Chapter Eleven

Kate held Jen's hand beneath the faucet, running warm water over the deep scratches left by Rufus, who now reclined on the back of the couch as if nothing out of the ordinary had taken place. Gently, she pumped some soap from the dispenser and rubbed it over the cuts.

"I wish I had some sort of stronger disinfectant," she said, hoping the antibacterial soap would be enough.

"I've had worse and been okay." Jen gave her a reassuring smile, then winced as Kate applied another pump of soap. Jen's hand was warm and oddly vulnerable like this, held out for Kate's inspection. The deep red lines glared up at them both.

"Does it hurt?"

"Not too badly. I can still use it." Jen flushed when she finished speaking, and a wave of heat overtook Kate at the insinuation, however unintentional. She shut off the water and reached for a paper towel, gently patting Jen's hand dry. The paper towel reddened with each soft dab.

"There," said Kate. She lifted Jen's hand to her mouth and kissed the torn flesh.

"Kate—"

She looked up, lacing her fingers through Jen's, to see Jen staring at her mouth with longing. Power swelled in her veins. Jen's desire was a drug, and Kate's system was already overloaded with the stress of the last few days.

"Yes?"

"Let me cook for you."

Not what she expected, but she stepped closer to Jen and placed Jen's hand on her hip, slipping hers free. "You don't have to do that."

"I want to." Jen pulled her closer. If the scratches on her hand bothered her now, it didn't show.

Kate brushed the short hair on the sides of Jen's head with her fingertips, enjoying the velvet sensation. She let her nails barely scratch Jen's skin. When had this woman come to mean this much to her?

"You go sit with your cat," said Jen. "I'll see what's in your kitchen."

"You sure I can't help? What if you can't find something?" Kate asked, the idea of Jen rummaging through her kitchen inducing both anxiety and a fierce affection.

"Then I'll call for help."

Thirty minutes later, Jen sat Kate at her own table with a glass of wine and a pasta dish full of the vegetables in the fridge and some sausage she'd forgotten about, plus some seasoning Kate hadn't realized she owned—or at least hadn't realized could be used like this.

"Oh my god," she said after taking a bite. "You cook, too?"

"I have to eat," said Jen.

"This is incredible." She took another voracious bite. She hadn't eaten much since Rufus had gone missing, and her appetite roared to life. Jen watched her eat with that damnable grin on her face. Kate didn't mind. She liked cooking well enough, but hated being the only chef in the kitchen. If Jen cooked regularly, then Kate would never let her go.

"Thank you again for everything with Rufus," Kate said.

Jen set down her fork. "You don't have to thank me. I was just happy I could help."

"I *want* to thank you."

"Kate," said Jen, reaching for her hand, "I want you to take my help for granted. I will be here when you need me, no matter what the problem is—that's a promise."

The sincerity in Jen's voice warmed Kate even more than the food, and she held Jen's gaze. "I'll never take you for granted."

"But you know what I mean, right?"

Kate did. Jen was promising her consistency and faith, and Kate loved her for it.

Loved? Oh dear.

"Also," Jen continued, "there's something I want to give you. Come by the forge tomorrow?"

The door to the forge was open when Kate arrived the next day, and she understood why once she set foot inside. Hot air blasted her face. Her wool coat felt too warm, and she began to unbutton it as her eyes roved the forge to land on Jen.

Good lord.

Jen stood in a battered pair of jeans slung low over her hips and a sweat-darkened heather-gray tank top, her gloved hand stoking the coals. Sweat trickled down her arms. Kate's hands stilled on her jacket. The tank top clung to Jen's abs, and the imagined sensation of running her fingers along that hot, wet skin seared up her arm and down into her belly. Kate hadn't seen anything this goddamn gorgeous in her life.

Jen grinned when she looked up. "Hey."

Kate swallowed. "Hi." Her jacket hung half open. She finished unbuttoning the last few buttons with clumsy fingers and hung the coat on a hook by the door next to Jen's. Warm air seeped into her long-sleeved T-shirt. She'd be too warm soon, but for right now the air felt good after the chill of early November. Jen set down the tongs and wiped her forearm across her forehead. The motion emphasized her biceps. Kate approached her slowly, letting her eyes roam up and down Jen's body. Desire misted the corners of her vision. Jen looked like she was in her element here, and Kate needed to feel the heat of Jen's hands on her bare skin. She wanted Jen to stoke her until she, too, burst into flame. She'd been so exhausted from Rufus's ordeal that she'd fallen asleep on Jen the night before, but her body still remembered the way Jen's hands had felt through the lace of her bra the night Jen had pulled back, and it needed more.

"I've got something for you." Jen pulled off her gloves one at a time and turned to grab the "something" from her workbench, giving Kate a view of her bare shoulders. The shop lights glimmered on her slick skin. Kate could almost taste the clean sweat, and her heart began pounding heavily. Jen looked incredible like this. Kate closed the distance between them and ran her hands down Jen's arms, savoring the way they glided. Jen shivered and looked over her shoulder, a crooked grin tilting her lips.

"I'm so sweaty right now," Jen said, as if this were a bad thing.

"I know." Kate kissed the back of Jen's neck and licked the damp skin. Jen shuddered again and braced herself on her workbench as Kate slid her hands beneath the wet tank top.

"Kate—"

"Hmm?" Kate brushed her fingers across Jen's abs, then dug her nails in, pressing herself against Jen's ass. Jen's breath hissed through her teeth.

"You are a safety hazard," Jen murmured as she tensed beneath Kate's fingers. Kate dragged her nails out toward Jen's hips, then down the small of her back. When she reached the hem of Jen's shirt, she lifted it, and Jen snatched it from her to tear it off over her head, turning around.

Kate wanted to crash into her, but the sight before her eyes was too incredible to rush. Jen's black sports bra cupped her breasts, and sweat beaded the line of cleavage. Kate traced it with a fingertip and brought it to her mouth, tasting the salt with the tip of her tongue.

"Christ," said Jen. Her hands were on Kate's hips before Kate realized Jen had moved, and she was lifted bodily onto the workbench as Jen shoved the assortment of metal objects and tools to one side before lifting Kate's shirt over her head and tossing that, too.

Hot air warmed Kate's skin instantly. She reached for Jen, but Jen was already there, crushing their mouths together with a groan. Callused hands squeezed her waist as if they couldn't get enough of the feeling.

Jen was normally so gentle. Her loss of control was a heady thing. Kate licked deep into Jen's mouth, tasting her and teasing her. She loved the way Jen's soft lips moved over her own, firm and sure, and when Jen's tongue tangled with hers, she loosed a moan. She wanted Jen deep inside her. *Now.* She broke the kiss to lick Jen's jaw and down her neck, earning her Jen's fingers on the waistband of her jeans as Jen undid the button.

"Can I—" Jen broke off as Kate nipped the muscle at the base of Jen's neck. It gave deliciously beneath her teeth. She did it again, sucking hard enough to bruise this time. Jen swore. Insistent tugging made Kate lift her hips enough for Jen to shimmy her out of her jeans, but she didn't stop tasting Jen. Her skin was addictive. She loved the way it felt under her tongue, and she loved, too, the way Jen hauled Kate's bare legs back around her waist, rubbing up and down her thighs. The scratch of her calluses sent goosebumps over Kate's body. She pressed into Jen's belt buckle, seeking friction.

"Can I fuck you?" Jen finished her sentence this time, whispering into Kate's ear. Kate's eyes fell shut as she gasped at the sensation of Jen's hand on her breast, her thumb brushing the nipple as she kneaded and stroked Kate through the green lace of her bra.

"Please." The word escaped on a pleading note Kate knew sounded desperate, but she was more turned on right now than she'd been in years, and didn't have a single fuck to give. "Please, yes."

Jen bit Kate's neck. She cried out as the sensation ricocheted down her body, bucking her hips and sending a fresh flood of desire between her legs. Jen did it again, devouring her with sweeping licks of her tongue in between nips until Kate's hips twitched with need. Jen's hands paused at the thin band of her underwear.

"Jen—"

"You're so fucking gorgeous," Jen murmured into the curve of her neck.

"Please—" She couldn't finish her plea. Jen slid her hand between them and into Kate's lingerie, palm and fingers hot against her. Kate arched, seeking anything Jen would give her.

"Fuck, Kate." Jen slid her fingers through the wetness she'd created, wonder in her voice. One of her fingers flicked the tip of Kate's clit.

"Oh god." Kate dug her nails into Jen's shoulders and shuddered. Sweat was beading on her own skin in the heat of the room.

"Do you like—" Jen started to ask, but Kate saw where the question was headed and beat her to it.

"Please go inside me," Kate begged. Jen slipped two fingers into Kate and curled them, her thumb pressing tenderly down on Kate's clit as she slowly began to pump her arm. A low moan traveled from the base of Kate's spine up and out over her lips. Jen filled her perfectly. She tightened around Jen's hand and leaned back on the bench for leverage, looking up at Jen.

Jen was staring at Kate's chest. Kate glanced down to see her breasts rising and falling rapidly, enclosed in her favorite thistle-patterned bra. She couldn't blame Jen—even she could appreciate the view. Jen's biceps tensed as she worked Kate over. Strong women had always undone her. And Jen—Jen was strength and softness all at once. Jen's dark eyes flickered to hers. Kate held them even as her mouth dropped open on another moan, Jen moving faster now, finding Kate's rhythm.

"Jen—" Her hips rose from the bench, and Jen supported her with her other arm, holding her up while she sent wave after crashing wave of pleasure up Kate's throat. It wasn't enough. She wanted all of Jen, everything she had to give. She felt starved even as Jen filled her because she'd always want more of this, always—

She cried out wordlessly, shuddering around Jen's hand.

Jen kissed her, then moved her lips down Kate's collarbones

and heaving chest, over the soft curve of her stomach, and down further still, kneeling before her on the shop floor. The forge burned behind her, and heat distorted the air that backlit Jen's head with ripples and eddies.

"I've wanted to taste you for fucking ever," Jen said, her fingers still and steady inside Kate. Aftershocks rocked her foundation, eliciting pulses of pleasure so intense it bordered on pain.

"Yeah?" Kate managed.

Jen didn't answer. Her eyes had closed, brows creased, and she repeated the motion. Kate bucked. It was too much, too strong—

Jen slowly licked the base of her clit, dragging her tongue in swirling circles, always just missing the bundle of nerves at the top. Kate relaxed into the sensation as her body recovered from her first orgasm. Jen hardly looked winded. Desire mounted again, chasing itself after Jen's teasing tongue until Kate shifted her hips, trying to get Jen to touch her where she needed it. Jen's eyes opened, hooded and wicked, and she curled her fingers as she sucked Kate's clit into her mouth.

Kate squeezed her thighs against Jen's head, unable to stop herself. The metal piercings in Jen's ears were the only cool things on her body. Jen laughed as Kate's grip tightened. The sound rumbled against her and Kate reached for something to grab, anything, settling at last on her own hair.

"Fuck," Jen swore. Her free hand rested beneath Kate's ass, which Jen squeezed as she sucked and licked and teased, leaving Kate a writhing mess. Jen was an undertow—irresistable. Kate's second orgasm built in wavelets. Each time she chased it, however, Jen stopped, pulling her clit between her teeth and holding it there.

"I didn't know you were a fucking tease," she managed to pant.

"Mmm," said Jen, not breaking her rhythm. Kate didn't know what that sound meant and didn't much care. Her legs trembled and her elbows shook with the effort of holding herself up and the rising oblivion Jen's mouth promised. Each cresting wave rose higher than the last. Jen got her close again, then eased off, and Kate screamed.

That seemed to have been what Jen was waiting for. She curled her fingers inside Kate, sucking on her clit while she rolled the tip beneath her tongue. Kate let go.

Jen didn't want to pull out of Kate. The aftershocks, delicate and addicting, fluttered against her fingers as Jen kissed Kate's thighs. She wanted to make Kate come again and again and again. Slowly, she kissed Kate's clit, testing her sensitivity. Kate shuddered. Jen loved that involuntary motion. She loved everything about this woman.

She loved Kate.

It felt too soon to say it, but she could show her. Gently, she eased out of Kate's warm, wet body, replacing her fingers with her mouth.

"I don't think I can—"

"Just relax," Jen said, dipping into her tart entrance. "I only want to taste you."

Kate whimpered and offered no further protests. Her chest was flushed and her eyes bright as they held Jen's. She'd never looked lovelier. Jen slid her hands beneath Kate's ass and lifted her closer to her mouth. Seeing her like this, giving in to complete abandonment—this was everything. Jen could watch Kate come a thousand times and it still wouldn't be enough. Sweat dripped down her back. The memory of Kate licking sweat from her skin pulsed deep in her abdomen as she coaxed another moan out of Kate. One of the straps of Kate's bra had slipped down her shoulder.

"Wait," Kate said, resting a hand lightly on Jen's head and struggling to sit up. "I want to do something for you."

"You did," said Jen, who was reluctant to relinquish her current position. She licked Kate's clit again in the hopes of distracting her. Kate, however, wrapped Jen's ponytail around her hand and gently drew her head back—which was hot.

"Please?" Kate leaned in to give Jen a languid kiss. "Tell me what you like."

"Whatever you want to do to me is fine by me," said Jen. It was the most honest answer she could give. She had preferences, yes, but right now she wanted to make Kate happy.

"Anything?" Kate pulled away and smiled coyly. "But you don't know what I could be into."

"I don't care." God, but she was turned on. She didn't resist when Kate lifted her sports bra over her head.

"Fuck," Kate breathed when she pulled back to stare at Jen's chest. The word slid across Jen's skin like a caress. "Take off your pants."

Jen obliged her this, too, stepping out of her boots and jeans until she stood in her briefs in the middle of her forge, the heat of the fire at her back.

"Those too."

The briefs joined her jeans.

"Give me one second." Kate hopped off the table, surprising Jen, and crossed the shop floor in her stocking feet to—turn off the light? Jen blinked in the near darkness, but the coals of the forge bathed the room with a warm red glow. In that half-light, Kate looked darkly mysterious, her hair black against the shadows of the walls, the thin fabric of her underwear a shadow on her skin. Jen hadn't taken it off, merely pulled it aside, because it looked too damn good on. Jen watched Kate approach her at a slow walk, mesmerized. It was easy to be mesmerized by the way Kate moved, the sway of her hips a pendulum Jen couldn't look away from.

"Anything?" Kate asked when she stood before Jen again. She ran her nail down Jen's sternum and between her breasts, then trailed it across her ribs, walking around Jen in a circle to stand behind her. Jen shuddered, her skin hypersensitive to Kate's touch. Kate brushed both hands over her shoulders and down her arms. "I can't believe you're real, sometimes," Kate murmured.

"Look at you. Jesus."

Jen laughed. Kate's hands returned to her back, exploring the dip of her spine and the muscles spanning her shoulder blades with a featherlight touch. It was driving Jen insane, but she held still, letting Kate explore her body. Kate's hand fell to Jen's ass and traced the cleft, and Jen couldn't help the sound that escaped her mouth. Fuck, but that felt good. Kate repeated the motion and Jen wished she had something to brace herself against. Instead, she closed her eyes as Kate's nails trailed down the backs of her thighs.

Warm breath teased her skin, and then, sweet Jesus God, Kate licked her from the apex of her thighs to the base of her spine, sending a deep jolt straight to Jen's clit. Jen couldn't take any more of this. She spun, pulling Kate to her feet, and kissed her deeply, her hands wandering over Kate's body as if she hadn't just devoured her. Her full ass, her curvy hips, the arch of her ribcage and the taste of her mouth—how would she ever recover from this? She walked Kate back toward the bench, intent on pinning her there again, when Kate dropped to her knees before her.

Jen froze. Kate's hair cascaded down her back as she looked up at Jen, her mouth a dark line across her face, her eyes gleaming with reflected light. She looked like a wild thing, and Jen never wanted to look away.

"Can you stay standing?" Kate asked. There was nothing for Jen to grab; Kate knelt between the bench and Jen. She nodded. Could she? They'd find out. Fuck. Kate looked so good on her knees, though Jen worried about the cold cement floor. Before she could say something about that, though, Kate slid her hand between Jen's legs and nudged them apart, letting her fingers tease Jen as she withdrew. The shock of contact sent another shudder through her. She rested one hand gently on Kate's hair.

Kate's breath warmed her as Kate hovered just above Jen's clit. "Do you like penetration?" Kate asked, her eyes lifted to Jen's. Jen nodded. It was all she could manage.

"Good," said Kate, and then she lifted Jen's leg over her shoulder—Jen was just able to brace her foot against the workbench—and plunged her tongue into Jen, reaching as deep as she was able, and Jen's hand fisted in Kate's hair. She hoped it didn't hurt. She didn't have control of the response, and control was not forthcoming, as Kate proceeded to lick her with obscene slowness, her tongue traveling the length and breadth of Jen's clit until she thought she might scream. When Kate came to the tip at last, she placed a featherlight touch, smirking as Jen's hips jerked.

"Tease," Jen muttered through an embarrassingly breathy exhale.

"Am I?" Kate drew a tight circle around Jen, spiraling ever tighter until, at last, she ran her tongue where Jen needed her. And again. And again. Jen wasn't sure she could stay standing after all. Both her hands were now buried in Kate's hair, and she stared as Kate's back arched with each sweep of her tongue. How was this woman real?

"Tell me what you like," Kate murmured as she slid her hand up Jen's inner thigh and stroked her opening.

"That," Jen managed. She appreciated Kate's commitment to communication, she really did, but she could barely form a thought right now, let alone voice a preference. Anything Kate did felt good.

Kate slipped a finger inside her, testing her resistance. There wouldn't be much, not with Jen this wet. Kate groaned against her and inserted another finger, thrusting gently as she—holy fuck—sucked Jen's clit deep into her mouth, pulling and sucking, her head bobbing back and forth and *fuck* that felt good. Jen staggered. Kate didn't relent. If anything, she sucked Jen deeper, drawing blood to her clit and raking the tip of her tongue over the tip as mercilessly as Jen had done to her.

She was going to fall over. She couldn't take this. Her legs trembled and her breath grew ragged as she clung to Kate, her head falling forward and her abs clenching as her whole body trembled.

"Christ, I—"

Color exploded in her vision as Kate brought her to the edge, holding her there as Jen rode her face harder than she meant to, but god, Kate's mouth.

She collapsed against the workbench when Kate pulled out of her. After a moment she helped Kate stand, reaching down to brush any debris off her knees for her.

"You're way too fucking good at that," Jen said, cupping Kate's face in her hands and kissing her hard. She wanted to be gentle with Kate, tender, but she couldn't help the strength of her need. She wanted Kate too much for tenderness.

"Is that a complaint?" Kate asked when Jen pulled away to let them breathe. That little self-satisfied smirk was back on her lips. Jen loved it.

"Never." Jen wrapped her arms around Kate and held her close. "You're perfect."

"You're only saying that because I just made you come," Kate teased.

"No." Jen fumbled around the workbench with one hand, looking for the package she'd set there earlier but unwilling to release Kate. At last her scrabbling fingers found the brown paper, and she held it up between them. "For you."

"What is it?" Kate asked, making no move to escape Jen's arms.

"You have to open it."

"But I like it right here," Kate murmured into Jen's ear.

"So stay." She linked her hands behind Kate's back so that Kate could lean away from her enough to handle the package without needing to step back. Supporting Kate like this felt good. Incredible. She couldn't wait to feel Kate's weight on top of her. The bed in her RV was far from glamorous, but she had plans for it. And Kate beneath her—the things she could do to her. *For* her.

"Jen, is this—?" Kate had torn away the paper. In the dark Jen could barely make out the shape of what she'd made, but she didn't want to move to get the lights. Kate turned in her arms so that the firelight was at its best advantage. Her fingers traveled the curve of the nautilus shell in a slow spiral.

"A serpentstone," Jen confirmed. She'd forged it over the last few days, discarding the first few attempts until she was happy with the result.

Kate didn't say anything for so long Jen began to worry she'd made a mistake. Then Kate looked up at her, tears shining on her face and a smile wide enough to crack Jen's heart in two.

"No one has ever made anything like this for me before."

"They should have," said Jen. Anyone who squandered Kate in their life was an idiot and deserved to lose her. "I'd give you anything."

"Is that still the orgasm speaking?" Kate's voice was teasing, but Jen sensed a note of insecurity beneath it and raged at whatever circumstances had ever made Kate feel like she wasn't enough.

"Kate," Jen said, stroking Kate's tear-stained cheek with her thumb. Kate's lower lip quivered and she bit it as if that might stop the tremor. Jen tapped that lip once with her thumb. "Maybe it's too soon and I'm an idiot for saying it, but it feels like I'd be lying to you if I didn't."

Jen paused to breathe, her chest tight with nerves. She couldn't walk this back once she'd said it. She couldn't unsay these words. She was also half convinced she might drown under the weight of them, and there was Kate, waiting expectantly.

Fuck it.

Jen took another steadying breath. Kate's eyes burned into hers as if she already knew what Jen was going to say, though Jen was too jittery to parse her reaction. It was, she realized, already too late to walk this back.

Forcing herself to speak slowly and surely, she finally said the words that had been haunting her. "I love you."

Hands pulled her face to Kate's and now it was Kate crushing their lips together, the metal ammonite pressed against Jen's cheek where it still lay in Kate's hand. Would it brand her? She stroked the small of Kate's back. Jen fell in love too easily. She'd learned that about herself the hard way, but while she fell in love easily she did not fall in love often. This thing with Kate was rare and precious. It was fine if Kate needed more time before she felt the same way. Jen would wait.

"Not too soon," Kate said, breaking the kiss. "I realized it the other day."

Jen needed Kate beneath her, now.

"Then," she said, already shoving her feet into her boots, "can I please take you to a real bed?"

Outside, the autumn wind gusted over the eaves. Kate shivered and Jen could see goosebumps rising on her arms.

"And leave the fire? It better be worth it," Kate teased.

Jen grabbed her jacket from its hook and wrapped it around Kate's shoulders, nudging Kate's shoes toward her.

"We'll run," she said.

"Run?"

Grinning, Jen gathered up their scattered clothes and, dressed only in her boots, nodded toward the door.

"Race you?"

"You wouldn't." Despite the words, Kate's face lit with mischief, and she slid into her shoes without taking her eyes off of Jen's.

"You sure about that?"

Kate reached for her clothes and Jen took a step back toward the door, keeping them out of reach. As she'd hoped, Kate laughed, feigning frustration as she swiped for them again.

Without warning Kate darted past her for the door, still laughing, and burst out into the November night. Jen stumbled, careful to shut the door to prevent any drafts from stirring the dying coals, and ran after her.

Chapter Twelve

Kate stood in the foyer of the Georgian townhome, Cam at her side, appraising the freshly painted walls. The previous owners had painted over the original color scheme in preparation for selling, and a few traces of red snuck through the white paint in places along the trim. An easy fix.

"This is the one you want?" she asked Cam for the third time. "Because we need to put in a bid ASAP."

Todd's clients were also interested in the property, and while she hated the guy, she couldn't deny his negotiating skills. He loved sneaking in last-minute counteroffers.

"I could see it working," said Cam. "For now at least."

"Is that a yes?"

"Yeah." Cam spread their arms and spun in a slow circle. "I like it."

"Then we need to draft an offer. We can try to get them to negotiate on price. I'll see if they have any other offers on the table."

She called the listing agent while Cam wandered the property, brushing their fingertips over the countertops and walls as they went. Was Cam settling down? Kate wanted that for her twin if that was what Cam wanted, but it was a strange idea. She didn't have long to ponder it, however, because the agent picked up instantly.

"This is Hannah," she said.

"Hi, Hannah. Kate Kovaleski calling. My client is interested in 27 Oakshot. Do you have any offers on the table?"

"We do, but I'll be honest with you, it's a lowball. If your client meets the asking price, we could talk."

Kate hung up shortly after and found Cam in the bathroom, no doubt pondering where they would place their many hair products.

"Someone has an offer in," she announced, leaning against the bathroom door. Cam pulled a face at her in the large mirror. "It's low, or at least that's what the listing agent said."

"Is that a negotiating tactic?"

"Could be, but I don't think so. Hannah tends to tell it like it is. The asking price *is* high, though. We could counter with something just below."

"Is there any way to find out who the other offer's from?" Cam asked.

"Why?"

"Just curious." Cam's tone radiated innocence, which was, of course, suspicious.

"I'm not letting you bid high to spite Todd."

"It's my money."

"I think we should put an offer in just under asking price," she repeated. "It's not a contingency offer, which should make it attractive."

"Unless the other offer isn't a contingency either."

"Trust me, okay?" Kate asked, and Cam relented with a sigh.

"Fine. Let's do it now."

Kate could have submitted the offer remotely, but she chose to go into the office to do some sleuthing. Despite what she'd said to Cam, she wouldn't mind thwarting Todd, and, more importantly, she didn't want Todd thwarting her. Perhaps she would overhear something of use.

"Hey, Denise," she said as she walked into the building with Cam not long after. Todd's car wasn't there, but maybe that was for the best. Denise could be more forthcoming on her own.

"You must be Cam," Denise said, eyes lighting up. "I've been hoping I'd get to meet you."

"Then you've been misled." Cam flashed Denise a bright smile. "You must be Denise."

Kate waited for the pleasantries to be over before she raised the topic of Todd.

"How many offers do we have cooking right now?" she asked, trying to sound nonchalant as she leaned against the desk, avoiding knocking over the cup of pens with their business logo.

"Quite a few between you! It's looking like a good month for us."

"We're about to go put one in for Oakshot," Kate said, hoping to lead Denise to the chase.

"That's such a pretty one," said Denise. "Hannah's easy to work with, isn't she?"

"That's been my experience, at least."

Denise didn't take that bait, either, and began talking about some of the more difficult agents in the area, which wasn't entirely professional, so Kate excused them and settled Cam in a chair in her office. The boring beige walls wrapped them in quiet.

"This will take me a minute. Hang tight."

Cam drew their phone from their pocket and began texting, a little smirk on their lips.

"How's Danny?" Kate asked as she pulled up the documents she needed.

"Fine." Cam didn't look up. Kate was glad she couldn't see her twin's phone screen. She had a horrible suspicion the content was not safe for work.

"Uh-huh." Kate hid her own smile. Sure, things could get messy if Cam and Danny didn't work out, but it was cute seeing her twin caught up in someone, especially someone as genuine as Danny.

"Do you want to grab something to eat?" Cam asked when Kate finished the offer and sent it over.

"Sure, what did you have in mind?" Kate said, then held up a hand for silence as voices sounded in the lobby.

"Hannah, hi," Todd said loudly from beyond the closed door.

"Thanks for your call. Another offer, you said?"

Cam and Kate looked at each other, each paused in the act of throwing on their jackets.

"Let me check with my clients," he continued. "I'm sure we can come up with a better offer for you. Yes. Thank you so much, always good to work with you. Say hi to Paul for me."

Of course Todd knew Hannah's husband's name. As much as she hated him, he was good at what he did. He was also intentionally having this conversation where she could hear—she was sure of it. Bastard.

"Claire—" It sounded like he'd gone into his office and sat down with his door ajar. "Hi, how are you? Great, glad to hear it. Listen, there's been another offer, so we may need to think about upping our bid. Do you think you…" With an audible click, Todd closed his door, cutting off the conversation before he started talking numbers.

"What a fucking dick," Cam said into the silence. "No way I'm letting him get away with that."

Kate shook her head. As much as she shared that sentiment, it would come at her twin's expense, which might even be Todd's endgame. "We don't need to go into a bidding war if you don't want to. There are other properties."

"He's trying to intimidate my sister." Cam gave her a flat look. "Nobody gets to do that. Get me this house, Kate."

Kate picked up the phone and called Hannah. "Hello? I know we just spoke, but I wanted to emphasize how much my client loves the property. We're willing to counter any counteroffers. Mhmm. Yes, I'd appreciate that."

"What did she say?" Cam asked when Kate hung up.

"She promised to reach out before they accepted any other offers." Kate pulled her jacket on the rest of the way and nodded toward the door. "I have one other call I have to make real quick on the way if you don't mind."

"Why would I mind?"

"Because it's to HR. I'm reporting him for sexual harassment."

January in Maine was frigid as a general rule, and this evening was no exception. The wind howled around the eaves of the cabin, but inside, the heat from the woodstove filled the rooms with a genial warmth that seeped into Jen's pores. *Home.* She put the finishing touches on the charcuterie board, which she'd assembled on her new kitchen counter, and walked it to the living room of her cabin. She had furniture now. Real furniture.

"Oh hey, look who's been domesticated," Ollie teased.

Annie swatted her spouse. "She's always been domestic."

"That looks like nice cheese."

"She always chooses nice cheese!"

"Just let me give her a hard time, okay? It's fun." Ollie placed a kiss on Annie's cheek, mollifying her.

"Charcuterie boards are Lunchables for grown-ups," said Danny. "Not that I'm complaining."

"Should I have made pizza?" Jen raised her eyebrows at the assembled group: Ollie, Annie, Stormy, Danny, Cam, and Kate. Perfect Kate. They'd been together for two months, now, and she couldn't remember ever being this happy.

"No," they chorused together.

"Though you do make a mean pizza, and I went to culinary school so I would know," Ollie admitted.

Danny leaned forward with enthusiasm, nearly growling. "Gimme that cheese." Cam smirked, amused, which Jen thought was probably because they'd never seen Danny polish off a block of brie in a single sitting. If they had, they'd be inching away to higher ground.

"Let's do a toast first." Jen reached for her beer and raised her glass to Kate. Danny slunk back into her seat. "To Kate, for getting into graduate school."

"Holy fuck," said Stormy. "Why didn't you say anything sooner?"

"I just found out," said Kate.

"Is it in person?" asked Stormy. "You're not allowed to move."

"It's online." Kate's smile was shy. "I should be able to keep working and study at the same time."

"This one will make you snacks," said Danny, pointing to Jen. It was a fair accusation. She'd already planned out some of the snacks she'd make sure were kept on hand for study sessions, and had daydreamed about sitting beside Kate on the couch, flipping through *The Farrier's Journal* as Kate studied.

"Get it, girl," said Stormy. The others chimed in with their congratulations. Kate blushed but smiled through it, her eyes taking in the room with a ferocious hope her smile didn't dim. Jen sat beside her and put an arm around her shoulder, relishing the way Kate fitted against her. *These are your people*, she wanted to say. *You don't have to be lonely anymore.*

"You're too much," Kate protested. "All of you."

"Just wait till you taste the cake I made," said Stormy.

Kate shook her head with a smile. The motion brushed her bun against Jen's cheek, bringing with it the scent of shampoo. On the days Kate didn't spend the night, Jen burrowed against the empty pillow, inhaling that smell as deeply as she could. She always slept better afterward.

She scanned the room, taking in her friends nestled together in her cabin, and let her grin stretch across her face. This was what she'd always wanted: a home she loved, filled with friends and the woman of her dreams, who'd remained an amorphous shadow in her mind until the day Kate walked into the brewery. Yes. She could get used to this, though it was hard to imagine ever taking it for granted. Kate had slipped seamlessly into Jen's circle, fitting like the tongue-and-groove boards on the walls of her cabin. Her chest ached with contentment. Sure, relationships had their ups and downs, and she and Kate would have theirs, but she welcomed those challenges. As with horses, you could get through almost any rough terrain with enough patience, trust, and care.

A spluttering cough erupted from Danny. Cam patted her back while Stormy threw her head back to laugh, cuing Jen that she must have taken an overly ambitious bite of cheese.

"Speaking of domestic . . ." said Kate, lightly squeezing Jen's thigh as she addressed the group. "A toast to Danny, for being the one to finally convince Cam to go on a second date."

"I have totally gone on second dates before."

"But not a third," said Kate, and Jen heard the smugness in her voice. Cam scoffed but had no comeback lined up. Jen knew for a fact there had been more than three dates, and quite a few overnights, thanks to the lurid texts Danny sent her the day after.

"What can I say," Danny gasped, eyes watering as she recovered. "I'm a fucking delight."

"Thank you." Kate looked at Jen with those luminous eyes. "You really didn't have to do all this for me."

"I know," said Jen, kissing her temple. She loved the slight indent there, and the way her lips fit against it. "But I wanted to."

"How do you like your new place, Cam?" Ollie's question brought Jen's attention back to the conversation.

"Love it," said Cam.

"You have to have a housewarming," Danny said. "It's the rules."

"Well, I wouldn't want to break the rules. Sure. I'll have a party. A 'Fuck Todd' party."

"I'd rather not associate him with your home," said Kate.

"I'd rather run him over with my car," said Cam. "This way I won't go to jail."

Kate laughed and waved Cam's words away. Jen happened to agree with Cam about the car bit, but Kate was handling the situation. Adding her own fury to the fire wouldn't help. Still, she was glad they'd outbid Todd's clients on that house. Kate deserved a win.

"The house is gorgeous," Danny gushed, and Jen supposed Danny would know, seeing as she spent a fair amount of time there.

"Cam's happy," Kate murmured to Jen. "It's cute."

I'm happy, Jen considered saying, but decided it was too trite. Still, as she sat there with Kate beneath her arm and her friends around her, she couldn't help smiling. How incredible, that she could fit her whole world beneath this roof. Mabel shoved her snout under Jen's free hand, knocking her drink, and Jen set down her beer to scratch the dog behind the ears. They'd built this together. Their laughter had permeated these walls, and even when the house was empty, she could feel the solidity of their love. Her friends. Her family. Kate.

"Hey," she whispered into Kate's hair, tuning out the conversation. "I'm proud of you."

"You helped," said Kate.

"Nah."

"Yes, you did."

"Does that mean I can't be proud?"

Kate laughed, and Jen accepted her victory. Kate couldn't argue with that, and there was so much to be proud of: Kate had applied for and gotten into a graduate program for architecture, had finally lodged a complaint against Todd that had led to disciplinary action, though it sounded like he'd only be made to sit through sexual harassment training, and had helped Cam find the house of their dreams—despite Todd's attempts to sabotage the process. She was a rock star. Jen was lucky to be sitting next to her.

"I'm proud of you, too," said Kate.

"For what?"

"For this." Kate gestured at the cabin and their friends. *Their* friends. Jen hoped Kate saw Jen's people as her own. She wanted to share everything with her, and while she couldn't imagine a future where Kate wasn't in her life, she also knew these people would support them both were anything to happen.

"You helped," Jen pointed out. "You're part of this."

"I know." Kate traced a spiral over Jen's knee. The shape matched the ammonite tattooed on her wrist, the eternal line spiraling ever inward.

"I was thinking about something," Jen said, entranced by the motion.

"Yeah?"

"I have a spare key. To the cabin. If you want it."

Kate turned to face her, eyes wide with surprise. Danny was teasing Cam and Ollie in the background while Annie and Stormy laughed. Jen ignored them. Her stomach cramped with sudden nerves.

"Really?" Kate's expression softened. "Jen, I—"

"I don't want to pressure you—"

"I'd love that." Kate's smile erased Jen's worries. "If you're sure."

"I'm sure." And she was. She was sure about Kate the way she was sure about iron. One day she'd find the words to tell Kate this, but for now she could give her a key and a kiss and hope Kate could feel the currents running beneath.

"There's just one thing we have to figure out," said Kate. Jen waited, trying to figure out what she could mean.

"What?"

"How Mabel is going to react to Rufus."

Jen laughed, drawing the attention of the group, and with one more kiss to Kate's temple she rejoined the circle of their friends and let the warmth of their company drive away the cold.

Acknowledgments

Jen and Kate's story started off as a Patreon novella, and while it has changed in almost every respect since then, I owe a huge thanks to my patrons for their support. It means the world to me. The fact that this novella has changed for the better is due in large part to my editor, Kit Haggard, who helps me see through the mess of my first drafts to the story beneath, and to my early readers. Jules, thanks for reading it twice. My students are a continual inspiration—thank you for being your brilliant, compassionate, creative selves.

I am incredibly lucky to write for a press that believes in queer stories. Salem, Ann, Marianne—thank you for the work you do to keep queer independent legacy presses alive, especially in the current political climate. The more of our books they ban, the more we'll write. I also have to give a shout-out to the farriers I've had the pleasure of observing and working with over the years. Thanks for answering my many questions.

And last but never least, Tiff, thank you for your support, as always. You have all my love.

About the Author

Anna Burke is an acclaimed novelist recognized for bold, emotionally charged stories. Her work blends sharp prose with deep humanity, earning her a devoted readership around the world. She holds an MFA from Emerson College and teaches Creative Writing. When she is not writing fiction, she is an overly ambitious gardener and teacher. She and her wife live with their spoiled pets in the Berkshires.

Follow Anna Burke here:
Instagram | @ annaburkeauthor
Facebook | facebook.com/annaburkeauthor/
Patreon | patreon.com/annaburkeauthor

The 2024 Foreword INDIES Publisher of the Year Award was presented to Bywater Books for its twenty years of ushering in the "coming of age of queer literature."

"In a year when LGBTQ+ communities faced renewed attacks and the names of DEI efforts were sullied by those in power, Bywater Books remained firm in its commitment to publishing titles that celebrate queer existence and that embrace diversity. Their world-widening books make us laugh, make us cry, and stand as enduring testaments to the breadth of love and the human experience."

—Foreword Reviews

Bywater Books believes that all people have the right to read or not read what they want—and that we are all entitled to make those choices ourselves. But to ensure these freedoms, books and information must remain accessible. Any effort to eliminate or restrict these rights stands in opposition to freedom of choice.

Please join with us by opposing book bans and censorship of the LGBTQ+ and BIPOC communities.

At Bywater Books, we are all stories.

For more information about Bywater Books, our publishing mission, authors, and our titles, please visit our website.

https://bywaterbooks.com